THE
JOURNEY OF
LITTLE CHARLIE

The
Journey of
Little Charlie

CHRISTOPHER
PAUL CURTIS

THORNDIKE PRESS
A part of Gale, a Cengage Company

GALE
A Cengage Company

Farmington Hills, Mich • San Francisco • New York • Waterville, Maine
Meriden, Conn • Mason, Ohio • Chicago

Recommended for Middle Readers.
Copyright © 2018 by Christopher Paul Curtis.
Thorndike Press, a part of Gale, a Cengage Company.

Thorndike Press® Large Print Mini-Collections.
The text of this Large Print edition is unabridged.
Other aspects of the book may vary from the original edition.
Set in 16 pt. Plantin.

LIBRARY OF CONGRESS CIP DATA ON FILE.
CATALOGUING IN PUBLICATION FOR THIS BOOK
IS AVAILABLE FROM THE LIBRARY OF CONGRESS

ISBN-13: 978-1-4328-6144-5 (hardcover)

Published in 2018 by arrangement with Scholastic, Inc.

Printed in the United States of America
1 2 3 4 5 6 7 22 21 20 19 18

*Dedicated with love and respect
to the Curtii:
Habon, Ayaan, Ebyaan, and Libaan*

"A journey is called that because you cannot know what you will discover on the journey, what you will do, what you will find, or what you find will do to you."

—James Baldwin

Just outside of
Possum Moan, South Carolina
August 1858

❧ CHAPTER 1 ❧

The Best Critter God Made

I'd seent plenty of animals by the time I was old 'nough to start talking, but only one kind worked me up so much that it pult the first real word I said out my mouth.

And 'cording to the only folks who was there to witness the whole fuss, the word kept tumbling outta me o'er and o'er for more'n half a day.

Long 'nough for Ma and Pap to wonder if I'd banged my head on something and got tetched. Long 'nough for 'em to start looking 'round for something to tie 'crost my mouth to hesh me up.

I don't know what it was 'bout this critter that riled me so, 'cause when you holt it up next to other animals, there ain't that much that's spec-tac-a-lar 'bout it.

It ain't nowhere near's big as a b'ar. And

it can't knock the biggest, strongest man down with one swipe.

It ain't nowhere near's sly nor quick as a cat; it ain't no good at all at mousing nor catching holt of birds without a lot of help.

And it ain't got nothing as bad a rep-a-tation as a snake; it don't get nowhere near the 'mount of talking 'bout in the Bible that snakes do.

I'd seent all them critters and plenty more, but it wasn't till Pap set the puppy that growed up to be Pinky next to me in the dirt of the front yard that I said, "Dog!"

I guess I done more than just say it; it's tolt that I screamed, "Dog! Dog! Dog! Dog! Dog! Dog! Dog! Dog . . ."

Pap tells me, "Little Charlie, neither you nor the pup hadn't showed signs of being nothing but dour and gloomish, but when we put you one next to the other . . . well, sir, it was though someone struck a flint on gunpowder! Sparks flew; y'all both made noises that neither pup nor babe had ever made afore, all the while rolling and laugh-ing in the dust, then, like y'all had a talk 'bout it and took a vote, tore off in them woods together."

Which was shocking, Ma and Pap said, since I hadn't even started crawling proper.

Ma tells me, "We was worried sick 'bout

you, Charlie. Why, if I had a penny for each person what axed me if you was a dimwit, I'd be rich as George Washington! I don't know how many times I had to tell folks you was just a babe, and not five or six years old, that that was why you wasn't walking or talking."

I figger the real reason was I hadn't seent nothing worth talking 'bout till I seent Pinky, and nothing worth getting up and chasing after till that particular minute neither.

Ma said the way I chased after that puppy brung to mind this contraption she'd seent at a fair in the city of Charleston when she was a girl.

"A automaton," she called it. " 'Twas one-half fancy pocket watch, one-half tin can, and one-half little boy, and it moved jus' as stiff and wobblish as you done running after that puppy, Charlie."

I don't remember doing the talking, but the picture of that wiggling, squirming, wet-tongued, fat ball of fussing and fur is in my head so strong that it's something I'm-a be pondering 'bout for the rest of my days. And I'm a real big ponderer.

When me and Ma is working the fields and the time's dragging, I learnt to make myself think on things so's I won't go dim-witted. I seent what's happened to Ma, how she keep on chopping or digging or weeding without doing no thinking. I seent how if you keep working without doing no thinking in the field, it 'come a bad habit and you can't help but do it elsewhere too.

We look at it different.

She says the best way to get through working the fields is to make her head be still and quiet as a pond. I want mine to be a river crashing through a waterfall. I got to be thinking 'bout something or else my head'll pop.

That's how I figgered out why dogs has worked their way so far 'neath my skin; now that I'm older and had lots of chances to see and be 'round other critters, I think it come down to the eyes.

At that first meeting-up with Pinky, n'en one of us couldn't talk, but we traded looks and both seent something one in the 'nother. When I looked in that puppy's eyes, I seent myself looking back! Sure's if her eyes was mirrors or a couple of shined-up silver cups. Not jus' the 'flection of me, but something that said, "This here critter knows you."

And I knowed when she was looking in my eyes she seent the same 'zact thing.

It didn't take but a half a second, but that

look's what got us both to cavorting and carrying on so. And that's a look that no animal, other than a dog, has ever give me since.

No other animal and not very many people neither.

Stanky, whose ma was Pinky, had give birth to a litter of six pups and they all lived. After they was 'zactly forty-nine days old, Pap said me and him had to look 'em o'er to see if there was a hunting dog in the bunch.

Pap tolt me, "A good dog is the same as a good person; they's born that way, not made. Ain't no silk purse ever been made out of a sow's ear."

The pups was squirming and sliding o'er one the 'nother, carrying on something fierce, nipping at anything that moved, not caring if they was biting their brother or sister or even their own selfs. Jus' looking to get any kind of puppy meat that they could in them sharp pinnish teeth.

All their antics was first-rate nonsense to me.

I'd axed Pap, "But how can you tell if they's gonna be any good hunting when they's acting so coltish and foolish, Pap?"

"There's a couple ways we do it."

Pap brung one the wood crates out the

shed and set it on the forest floor behind the cabin. Then we brung the pups and put 'em inside the crate. They was still so small that they had plenty room to move 'bout.

Pap said, "I'm thinking it's that black one with the white spot on her tail. We'll see how good my eye is."

I couldn't let Pap know, but that one's name was Ashes.

When the pups had been first born, Pap got vexed with me once I started naming 'em. I couldn't unna-stand why, but he'd made me stop.

I named 'em anyway and kept it to myself.

"Keep a sharp eye on 'em and tell me what you see."

Pap had gone to the shed and brung out four of his bullets and his pistol. He kept 'em hid under the floorboards wrapped up in a fancy piece of thick purple curtain that had beautiful gold tassels sewed on 'long-side the fringe.

The curtain was well knowed throughout all of South Carol-liney. It was so fancy 'cause Ma had bought it offen a woman who is the cousin of George Washington. The woman tolt Ma that George give a whole set of 'em to his wife, Martha, for her birthday and Martha got vexed, saying George had gone cheap on her, paying only

five hunnert dollars 'stead of the five thousand dollars she was 'customed to having
spent on her. She couldn't 'bide having
nothing so common in her home and sold
the curtains to George's cousin for next to
nothing.

Ma had tolt me that meeting the woman
was a sign that the luck of the Bobos was
changing. She said in life, there was good
luck followed by no luck, followed by bad
luck, followed by tragical luck, followed by
the luck of the Bobos.

Pap reached in the crate and pult out the
first of the pups, Ashes. He flipped her on
her back and helt her down by her belly.

She squirmed for a second, then set still.

Pap kept her pinned down.

After a bit she began tussling to get set
free, even biting at Pap's hand.

Pap shook his head and smiled.

He done the same with each of the rest of
the pups.

Some of 'em fought like badgers to get up
soon's they was flipped, some of 'em jus'
laid there waiting to see what was gonna
happen. Curly and Nippy done the same as
Ashes.

Pap put 'em all back in the crate and
unwrapped the pistol out the curtain.

He loaded it up with four bullets and

17

raised it o'er his head.

I covered my ears.

Pap pulled the trigger and the forest shook from the boom.

Me and all six of them pups flinched.

Pap waited a second, then fired the next three bullets fast-fast.

Sagebrush, Ol' Thunder, and Squalane kept on flinching with each shot that come, then pressed theyselfs into the corners of the crate, whining and spinning in circles.

Ashes, Curly, and Nippy was different. They come to 'tention after that first flinch and was staring up at the gun with their front legs stiff as stone and their chests all bowed out and their eyes burning. Their ears was perked up and, 'stead of being scairt by the noise, they was looking for more of it. These was the same three that stayed still at first when Pap flipped 'em but soon tired of the whole thing and fought.

Ashes was even making a huffing sound, as though she wanted to bark but wasn't sure if she should.

I set to com-fitting the scairt puppies. I didn't want Pap to know I'd disobeyed his orders, so 'stead of using their proper names I didn't say nothing more than "It's all right, li'l pup" and "There, there, girl."

Pap laughed and shouted, "Man alive!

18

That ol' dog done birthed three hunters! Come on, boy; don't tell your ma, but once they's growed and I gets 'em trained, she gonna be getting a store-bought dress! And you's gonna be getting some proper shoes! Three hunters outta one litter! We'll keep one of 'em, and you get to decide which."

I didn't let another second get by; I said, "We'll keep the one with the white-tip tail!"

Pap didn't su-spect nothing. I said, "And I'm gonna call her Ashes," which only made sense since that was already her name.

Pap roughed up Stanky's neck and said, "What a dog!"

The next day, when me and Ma come out the field toward dusk, I was washing off at the pump. Soon's she seent me, Stanky starts up doing something she ain't never done afore. She gets to whining and rubbing herself 'gainst my legs, acting cattish!

I pushed her off twice, then on the third time, I was fixing to give her a good swat, but I seent how upset she was, so I helt up.

What come to mind was that one the pups must've got sick or maybe even died. Without drying off or nothing, I went 'round back of the shed to see if that's what got Stanky so jumpy.

I looked down in the crate where she kept 'em and couldn't believe my eyes. Only

Ashes, Nippy, and Curly jumped up to give me greetings. Sagebrush, Ol' Thunder, and Squalane wasn't nowhere to be seent.

I looked to the woods and whistled for 'em, but nobody answered.

"Where they at, Stanky?"

She kept looking at me all pitiful, whining and sniffing at the crate.

I tolt Ma.

She cut her eyes and said, "They probably done run off, Charlie. Or maybe they was sick and Stanky took 'em out in the forest to let nature have her way. I don't know, son, there's other things to fret 'bout. Let me scare something up for you to eat."

And even though I had my 'spicions 'bout what really happened to them three pups that had flinched with every shot, first thing after I woke up for two weeks straight, afore I went off to the fields, I'd stand behind the cabin and try whistling 'em up and calling 'em home.

I guess it mean ain't no doubt I'm a Bobo; I didn't have no luck at all.

CHAPTER 2

Time the Trickster

Time moves different when something you ain't 'specting to happen goes 'head on and happens anyhow. I seent where time goes from moving at the reg'lar pace to when it slides 'long on greased locomotive rails. I also seent where it slows right on down, like it's fighting its way through a big invisible jug of molasses.

Trouble is I can't never figger what it is that makes one thing move fast and the other slow.

For a sample, if you was to ax me afore I seent what happened to Pap, I never would've thought time could slow down in the way it done. It was something so turrible that I'd-a give anything to make it go by faster, or better still, make it so I didn't never see it at all.

21

As 'shamed as it make me feel and cold-heart as it sound, I wish I'd-a jus' run 'crost Pap laying at the foot of that old maple with that big gash setting like a extra smile 'crost his forehead.

If I hadn't been cursed to see what happened with my own eyes, it probably would've been nigh on useless to try and figger how my pap come to be laying there, but I'd trade being ignorant 'bout it in a hop, skip, and a jump if that meant the sight of him wouldn't be barging into my dreams no more.

But I seent it, and unseeing something's the same as unringing a bell; it ain't never been done. I don't care how much you want to get rid of the remembering, you might as well not fight it; you might as well jus' go 'head and make yourself a holster, 'cause that memory is yourn and you gonna be toting it 'round for the rest of your life.

I 'member the minutes after Pap got knocked down as though I was watching it happening to someone else.

It was like I was watching some other boy 'stead of me picking Pap up and going o'er to Spangler with my pa in his arms.

I 'member thinking right off how the boy wasn't gonna be able to get Pap on Spangler's back long as the saddle was there.

22

I 'member seeing the boy, who I knowed was me, laying Pap down soft on the ground and how Pap's eyes come open.

I 'member the boy closing Pap's eyes and taking the saddle offen Spangler and leaving it in a tree so's no one would interfere with it afore we come back.

I 'member the boy going and picking my pap back up and setting him 'crost Spangler's back near his neck so's Pap's head and arms was hanging off to the right and his legs was throwed off to the left.

I 'member watching the boy climb up on Spangler's back, being careful not to kick Pap when he throwed his leg o'er.

I 'member the boy finding jus' how fast he could go without causing Pap no distress, but at the same time trying to fly.

I 'member the way Stanky'd jumped up whining and crying during the whole trip to Doc's, licking at Pap's hand, which was dangling and swaying loose and limp 'long-side Spangler's belly.

I 'member how thankful I was when the boy got to Doc's house and fount him home.

I 'member the boy pulling Pap offen Spangler and cradling him and carrying him inside like a baby.

I 'member how Doc called for Petey the dimwit and Josh Bowen to come give him a *hand taking Pap away from the boy.*

Then I 'member sitting on Doc's couch, feeling I'd carried the weight of the whole world on my shoulders.

'Twasn't long afore the sheriff come in and axed me to explain how Pap had got hurt.

On the ride back from Doc's house, I wondered 'bout how I'd tell Ma what happened, but I'll be blanged if I couldn't think 'bout it for but a second or two afore I'd have to quit so's not to bust out in tears.

I was jus' gonna have to wait till I seent her and hope I'd find a way to say the words that I was sure was gonna jus' 'bout kill my ma.

The cabin was empty. Even though it was Sunday, Ma was probably out in the fields trying to get a leg up on the weeding.

Me and Stanky started walking off to where we'd finished yesterday at dusk.

She seent me from 'bout a half mile off and waved her arm twice o'er her head afore she got back to digging out weeds.

After while, she stopped weeding mid-swing and looked back up at me.

She stood straight up, shaded her eyes with her right hand, then threw the rake to the side and commenced running at me.

I don't know how she knowed so sure that

something was wrong. And wrong in a big way. But she knowed.

She started up yelling when she was 'bout fifty yards from me, "No! Charlie! What happened? Where's he at?"

Stanky ran out to Ma and commenced jumping and nipping at her. Ma swatted her away.

Ma got to me and set to slapping at me with both hands.

"What's I s'pose to do now? What's I s'pose to do?"

Stanky took to tugging at Ma's shift, trying to pull her offen me.

I was froze. Ma kept swinging and slapping as though it was me who'd done something to Pap. I didn't even bring my hands up to protect myself.

"I'm as good as dead! What am I to do?"

I tried wrapping my arms 'round her to pull her close, but that jus' got her more and more vexed. She closed her fists and went from slapping me in the chest to throwing roundhouses and jabs at the side of my head.

Ma is big-boned, same as me and Pap, and he always tolt me, "Your ma ain't no delicate flower of a woman." One or two of her mannish punches had me feeling wobbly and top-heavy.

Stanky had had 'nough of Ma's nonsense and went from tugging on Ma to working herself 'twixt us and going at Ma with more and more worrisome growls and the showing of more and more teeth.

Ma reared back to throw a jab right at my face. Afore it hit, though, Stanky jumped up and, careful as she could, grabbed holt of Ma's wrist and gentle pult Ma's arm down.

Ma tried shaking Stanky off, but Stanky wasn't having none of it; she bit into Ma's wrist harder and harder until Ma didn't have no choice but to quit going at me and start paying 'tention to the dog that was getting closer and closer to drawing blood or breaking a bone.

Ma falled into a ball and Stanky set in to doing that heavy rump shaking and tail wagging that dogs do when they's looking to 'pologize for something they done. She licked all of Ma's tears and wouldn't quit even though Ma kept trying to wave her off. Finally, Ma give in and took Stanky's bathing whilst weeping something turrible.

All I could do was stand next to 'em with my hands hanging down, big useless sacks-o'-nothing at my sides.

She said, "Thank goodness you's old 'nough to look after yourself."

I frowned and jus' 'bout said, "No, I

ain't," but thought better of it.

I could see I was gonna have to do a lot of pondering on this 'cause things couldn't get much worst with Pap laying dead and cold on a table in Doc's house and our world coming 'part at the seams.

CHAPTER 3

Snared!

It was hard telling one day from the next. The only thing that kept me and Ma from losing our minds was working in the fields. Whilst everything else 'round us was changing and hard to think about, the fields was always the same, always something you could count on.

Things got turned upside-around and 'stead of looking forward to sunset, I wished the sun would get stuck right at noon and stay there 'cause the fields was the only time I didn't start thinking 'bout Pap's undoing.

I don't 'member 'zactly how long it was afore I answered a knock at the door and was surprised to see Sheriff Jackson standing on the porch.

"Morning, Sheriff."

"Morning, Little Charlie."

The sheriff looked me up and down.

"I noticed the other day you done growed a lot, boy."

"Yes, sir."

He grabbed my arm and whistled. "You's stronger than most full-growed men, ain't you?"

"I don't think so, sir."

"Big as your arms is, it wouldn't take much for you to knock down a small tree with one swing, would it?"

"I ain't never tried, sir."

"Yup, big as your arms is, I bet it wouldn't."

Most times when someone's talking 'bout how growed and strong I look, I have to fight not to smile nor blush; them things jus' ruins the growed picture of me that my size paints and show I ain't nothing but a kid. But something 'bout all these questions the sheriff was batting 'gainst me felt different. Smiling nor blushing wasn't nowhere in my mind.

Sheriff Jackson said, "Little Charlie, I hope you won't mind riding 'long and showing me the place in the woods where this tragedy befell your pa."

The uneasiness that was churning 'round in my belly started making itself heavier.

Me and Pap had rode out miles afore he

spotted the maple he said would be perfect for finishing the cabinet we'd been working on for months for Mr. Dalton.

Then it hit me; we'd gone so far out that the tree Pap picked must've been on the Tanner plantation!

"Sheriff Jackson! Sir! I swear on my ma's head that we didn't know we was stealing no one's wood. Pap wouldn't never do nothing to rile up Mr. Tanner. We seent the whuppings he give to folks who's poached on his land. Pap wouldn't do nothing to cross him."

That was the swear-'fore-God truth. Pap had had a bad time out at the Tanners' with their o'erseer, Cap'n Buck, who was the man that done the whuppings we was all forced to watch.

Word would get sent out that everyone from all 'round the county need come to the Tanner plantation and watch the cap'n tear the hide offen some poor farmer who was 'cused of shooting one the Tanners' deers or pheasants, or fishing in the stream that run 'crost their land.

Pap said as harsh as Cap'n Buck was on the white farmers near the Tanner plantation, he was even worst on the slaves that dared cross him.

The sheriff grabbed my arm again and

said, "This ain't 'bout no wood stealing, boy. You best jus' come 'long with us."

Us?

I followed the sheriff out the front door and there was five mounted men waiting on me. Petey the dimwit was one of 'em and he was holting on to the reins of a old riderless mare.

This was a posse, a sad little one, but if you's seent a posse afore, it ain't hard to rec-a-nize one the second time 'round.

I said, "I can go get Spangler and ride him, sir."

The sheriff said, "Well, Little Charlie, if it ain't no trouble, why don't you climb on up next to Petey."

Now there wasn't no doubt, this was 'bout stealing wood! Why else would they have a posse already brung together? Why else would they think I was gonna try and run off and give me a lame horse so's I couldn't?

My legs turnt to stone. What if the punishment for stealing lumber wasn't getting whupped; what if it was to get hunged?

I looked for a way out, but there wasn't gonna be no escaping; the sheriff was smarter than he was letting on. I'd falled into his snare.

The way the posse was lined up had the sheriff and one the other men up front and me and Petey riding abreast in the middle whilst the other two men trailed behind.

Petey wouldn't look me in the eye whilst I clumb up on the horse's back. Me and him had us a falling-out a while afore and he was still vexed.

I give the reins a tug to pull 'em from his hands, but Petey snatched 'em back.

He yelled, "He's trying to bust loose, Sheriff Jackson! Can't one a y'all jus' go 'head and wound him?"

The sheriff said, "He ain't trying nothing, Petey. You remember what I said; we's all got a job here and yourn ain't nothing but to holt on to them reins."

Petey was real disappointed. He said in that whining singing-a-song voice of hisn, "Well, couldn't I jus' shoot him in the foot and we wouldn't have to worry 'bout him running at all?"

The sheriff clumb down from his horse and come back to Petey.

"Now you look here, Petey Timmons. You ain't got no pistol, do you? I tolt your ma you could ride 'long only if you wasn't carrying no weapon."

Petey reached in his coat pocket and pulled out this old six-shooter. He passed it down to the sheriff. The only thing on it that wasn't rusty was the wood grips.

"Sorry, Sheriff. Don't say nothing to Ma; she don't know I brung it. She don't even know I got one."

The sheriff looked the gun o'er, seent it didn't have no bullets and that the trigger was so rusty it wouldn't budge. He handed the piece of rust back to Petey.

Sheriff Jackson winked at me and said, "Listen here, Petey, you gotta promise me, if Little Charlie do try bolting, you gonna throw this six-shooter at him hard as you can."

That set the other men to guffawing and chuckling. Petey laughed right 'long with 'em, never knowing the joke was on him.

I showed 'em which way to head out.

For the next four miles that we was riding into the forest, my mind didn't come offen the hangman's noose once. Everything I ever 'membered 'bout folks hanging someone was running through my head o'er and o'er. Including the hanging of Jesse Huddleston that Mr. Tanner had made everyone come see.

After while the sheriff said, "You sure this the right way, boy?"

"It ain't far from here, sir. Can't no one blame us for not knowing the Tanner plantation come out this far, can they?"

"Naw, Little Charlie, I done tolt you this

ain't got nothing to do with no lumber steal-ing. From my reckoning, this here's Injun land. Jus' hesh up."

The feeling of relief that sprung up in my heart didn't rest there for more than a beat or two, 'cause if what the sheriff was saying was true, why was I being rode out here in the middle of a posse?

I seent the maple from 'bout a hunnert yard off.

I swallowed hard and said, "It happened right up there, Sheriff Jackson."

Them words was a bell a-tolling; my posse, which had got more tireder and more draggish with each mile we rode, perked up right and proper.

The two men that was following stopped slouching in their saddles and watched me sharp-eyed. Petey helt on to the barrel of his pistol and shook it at me like it was a hatchet, ready to cleave me clean in half.

We got to the tree and tears started well-ing up in my eyes. Pap's blood was still pooled up on the ground where he falled.

The sheriff turned in his saddle and said, "OK, Little Charlie, tell me once more 'gain 'bout what happened to your pa."

I was beginning to think the rep-a-tation the sheriff had 'mongst folks was wrong. Word is he's a good, honest, and mostly smart man, but to me he was showing signs of being a bit slow. This musta been the third time he axed me to tell what had happened to Pap.

I's real patient when I tolt him again. "Pap picks out this here maple as the perfect size and age. He got the big ax and sent me to pull some handsaws offen Spangler for trimming.

"I stops for a second to see how far Pap's gonna drive that ax in with his first blow."

Ma says the way Pap swings his ax is one of them things that makes life worth going through; says she probably wouldn't-a never married Pap if she hadn't run 'crost him in the woods, hacking hunks outta trees. Once she felt how the earth shook after Pap tore into a tree, she didn't have no choice but to marry him, 'cording to her. Which is peculiar, but what that growed folks do ain't?

I tolt the sheriff, "Pap raises the ax up, slides his right hand 'long the handle, takes two practice swings, then slams the ax at the tree like he's gonna knock it o'er into the next district."

That had been when time started moving slow, so slow that I didn't have no choice but to watch near everything.

I tolt the sheriff, "The ax whistled as Pap swung it at the tree, the sun hit it, and it wasn't nothing but a flashing silver blur. But then . . ."

My breath got snagged in my throat.

"Go on, boy."

"Then the ax hit the tree and 'stead of making that good solid booming chunk it always made previous, Pap's ax made the same sound the blacksmith does when he's using his hammer to bang a hot shoe on a anvil.

"Then the tree done the dangdest thing. Pap hit it so hard that it squeals and throws a ball of sparks and fire like it was 'bout to bust out in flame!"

The sheriff, who'd been listening and nodding his head, butted me off. "Right there, Little Charlie! Right there's one 'em things that don't make no sense. I ain't saying you lying, boy, but how in tarnation's a tree gonna throw sparks?"

"I don't know, sir, it jus' did. Then the ax handle come 'live; it shakes and cracks into long skinny splinters, Pap screams, and his hands come flying off the handle like it had turnt itself into a lightning bolt."

I ain't never afore heard Pap cry out from hurting. Even when his left little toe and the one next to it got sawed off by Doc without no kind of numbing and Pap hadn't made a peep.

Pap's cry was a powerful disturbing memory. Disturbing and fresh. It was part of what was making me jump out my sleep. It made me wish I was deef.

The tears started fighting their way back in my eyes, but I wasn't 'bout to let the dimwit and them other men see me cry.

I took a deep breath and pretended I was 'bout to cough.

"Then, sir, the head of the ax bounced off that maple clean and crisp as a flat stone skipping off a pond. It kissed itself off Pap's forehead with a horrible sound, then whistled on off into the woods."

Sheriff Jackson said, "It's important we find that axhead, boy. Which way did it go?"

"I didn't see where it went, sir; all I seent was how Pap's backbone went ramrod stiff, standing him straight as a soldier; he froze that way for a bit, then keeled o'er backward the same way a rotted-out hunnert-year-old oak would. Didn't nothing bend on him; he jus' falled straight back like his foots was hinged to the ground."

"Then what?"

"That was all, sir. I put Pap 'crost Spangler's back and rode fast as I could back to Possum Mo—"

The sheriff jumped my talking one more time. "That! That's another one 'em things that jus' causes questions to be raised, boy. You say you and your pa was out here alone?"

"Yes, sir."

"You and your ma didn't 'range for no one to be waiting in the trees?"

"*What?* Waiting in the trees? No, sir. Why would we —"

"Explain this to me, then, Little Charlie Bobo. Big Charlie, may his soul rest in peace, was six and a half feet tall and weighed three hunnert and fifty pound if he weighed a ounce.

"Ain't no doubt you's huge for your age, but folks is having the turriblest of times seeing how a twelve-year-old boy's gonna lift that much deadweight. 'Specially how you could lift your pa high 'nough to lay him 'cross the back of a horse? That's a job for at least two men. Two *big,* strapping men."

It hadn't never crossed my mind.

"I can't say for sure, sir. All I know was when I heard Pap cry out, then seent him still and quiet on the ground, staring into the heavens, something come o'er me that got me so scairt and worried that I'd-a done anything to help him, sir. So I bent o'er and picked him up. He didn't weigh nothing to me. Even if Spangler wasn't there, I could've run all four miles back with him in my arms."

The sheriff said to the three men and Petey, "Y'all get on down from them horses and start looking 'round for that ax-head."

He turned back to me. This time when he talked, he'd quit being so mad at me.

"Son, you got to understand why we got questions 'bout what happened out here. There wasn't no witnesses and . . . well . . . to be blunt, word's going 'round that your pa had come into some money and was fixing to run off to Cincinnati with . . ."

The sheriff looked mighty discom-fitted.

"Well . . . with someone who wasn't your ma. You saying you didn't know nothing 'bout that?"

It wouldn't-a been no more surprising if Spangler sprouted wings and flew off to scare mice under the queen of England's chair!

Pap running off to somewhere called Seen-Seen-At-Eee?

The sheriff seent his words knocked me into a cocked hat.

He said, "We also heard there was some sharp talk and some blows passed 'twixt your ma and pa at the Tanners' store in the past weeks. What was it that got your ma so vexed at him?"

He was right. Ma was sore disappointed that the store wouldn't give us no more credit until we paid down on what we owed. She started going at Pap 'bout how come he ain't been paying what he was s'pose to and how close us and our animals was to starving and how she shouldn't-a never married him.

"Yes, sir, Ma was right vexed with him. I didn't have no feelings one way or the 'nother. I knows best than to put my nose in growed folks' business."

The sheriff said, "Little Charlie, you put them things together and even Petey thinks it's fishy that your pa was kilt right after him and your ma near come to blows. Especially out here in the wilderness with no one to say what really happened."

What *really* happened?

How plug-stupid could I be?

The sheriff *was* fitting my neck for the noose, all right, but it wasn't for stealing none of Mr. Tanner's lumber. He was looking to prove I'd murdered my own pap!

There wasn't a whole lot of talking done when the posse took me home. But the sheriff did make Petey turn a-loose the reins of the lame mare I'd rode out on and give 'em to me. I guess if I got the urge to bust

40

loose now, me and the lame mare could waddle and limp our way into the woods.

When we got to our cabin, the sheriff said, "OK, Little Charlie, I wants Judge Byrd to go out with me and look at that area. Y'all ain't planning on going nowhere, are you?"

Where would we go? In all my twelve years, I ain't never been more'n ten mile from Possum Moan.

"No, sir, we ain't got no plans but to get back into the fields."

"Good boy, Little Charlie. Tell your ma we'll be getting back with y'all."

"Yes, sir. Good-bye, sir."

Judge Byrd was knowed as the smartest man in the county. He quit being a judge so's he could do all Mr. Tanner's courthouse work for him.

My only hope was that he'd find something that would clear my name and keep me from swinging from a limb with a stretched neck and tied-up feet.

A week crawled past after Sheriff Jackson and his posse took me to the woods, and in that time, me and Ma and Stanky done jus' as I tolt him we was gonna and spent all our time in the fields.

'Twas getting near harvesting time and we couldn't waste one minute, else we might not get the crops in.

❧ CHAPTER 4 ❧

Wiggling out the Noose

Ma had heard that the sheriff, Judge Byrd, and some other big bugs had gone back out to look at the tree to try and get 'nough proof to put me away. Folks tolt her the only reason I hadn't got throwed in jail yet was the big bugs was too busy arguing if I should get strung up or jus' locked 'way for the rest of my life.

It was with a lot of fear in my heart when, after hours in the fields, a gentle knock at the door caught me just afore I was 'bout asleep. 'Twas peculiar 'cause it was long after sunset and most folks was at home looking to rest for tomorrow's work.

I looked out on the porch and whispered to the other side of the curtain that divides the room, "Ma? You sleeping? It's the sheriff!"

Ma whispered back, "Tell him I'm right out my mind with grieving and ain't talking nor thinking straight."

I heard her covers rustling, then she whispered, "If they here to arrest you, don't put up no fight, Charlie. I'll come visit you in jail soon's I can. It might not be for a spell; all this kerfuffle's got me so worked up I'm thinking 'bout going on o'er to May-May's for a while.

"But don't worry, I'll come afore too long."

She started doing a bogus snore.

I opened the door.

I was half 'specting to see shackles and a pulled six-shooter in Sheriff Jackson's hands, so I was took aback when I opened the door and he's holting his hat in his right hand and a burlap sack in his left.

He said, "Evening, Little Charlie. Is your ma about?"

I tolt him, "I'm sorry, Sheriff Jackson, but Ma ain't in her right mind and I'm the only one that's left to tend to her. If I was to go somewhere for any time at all, I'm 'fraid she'd die right off. The one time she come to and talked some sense, she said if someone took me 'way from here, her death would be on that person's hands. Don't matter how good a rep-a-tation the person has. He might as well jus' go right in and stick Ma with a Bowie knife 'cause by taking me away he'd sure be killing her."

Sheriff Jackson said, "Calm down, son. I understand. I ain't looking to do nothing to stab no one in the heart; I don't even own a Tennessee toothpick."

He cleared phlum outta his throat, then says, "Little Charlie, I'm sore sorry 'bout what y'all's gone through. 'Cluding what I done to you out in 'em woods."

He reached up to put his right hand on my shoulder and said, "Come on outside if you don't mind, Little Charlie. You and me needs to do some straight talking and I don't want to disturb your ma."

I still wasn't too sure if this might be him getting ready to bushwhack me.

He'd already snared me once; I wasn't looking to get tricked again. There could be shackles in the sack and Petey could be hiding outside the door, peeing his pants for the chance to yell, "You's under arrest, boy," afore he used that rusty pistol to bust my skull open.

I followed the sheriff onto the porch and was complete relieved when he put his hat back on, reached into the sack he was carrying, and pult out a roundish flat stone; 'twas 'bout two inch thick and as big as a smashed muskmelon. It would've been a perfect skipping stone if you was a giant.

He set the sack on the porch and it made a peculiar thud sound.

"I needs to talk to you man-to-man, Little Charlie."

Relief lightened my load 'cause I wasn't 'bout to get hunged, but this was one 'em times I wish I wasn't so big and tall; he was 'bout to say something that he wouldn't say if I was the size I'm s'pose to be. I sure wasn't looking forward to his next words.

"Little Charlie Bobo, some the time, responsibility gets put on us when we think we ain't ready for it."

I didn't say nothing.

"So that means you gonna have to be the man of the family now. It ain't gonna be easy, but I done talked to lots of folk what sends their best and say they's gonna give y'all a hand till y'all's able to get back on your feet."

Pap says Sheriff Jackson's one 'em people that take all the talk about not bearing false witness to heart. Says the man ain't got many friends 'cause he don't have no idea that a good lie tolt at the right time can go a long way to soothing folks' ruffled feathers.

Pap's words was true.

The sheriff slapped his hat on his knee and said, "Well, doggone it all, boy, they *saying* they's willing to give y'all a hand, but knowing them folks, I wouldn't depend on much more than a bowl or two of tater salad and maybe a couple of shoes for your horse.

"What I'm saying, Little Charlie, is y'all ain't gonna have much time to mope 'round and mourn; you best start looking to hiring yourself out. If y'all's to fall behind on what you owe Mr. Tanner, I ain't gonna have no choice but to evict y'all. Them Tanners don't care one whit what kind of grieving y'all's in the middle of. I sure wouldn't want to do it, but my hands is complete tied."

He never looked at me the whole time he was talking. Then he looked up in my eyes and said, "But I don't want neither one of y'all looking for no work on the Tanner place; don't no one need to get involved out there."

I cleared my throat and said, "Thank you, sir, I 'preciates the advice."

He helt up the stone.

"The Lord sure do work in mysterious ways, Little Charlie. If your pa had struck that blow a foot higher or a foot lower, wouldn't nothing have happened; he'd-a come home and et supper same as any other day."

The stone Sheriff Jackson was turning o'er and o'er had one big chip right out the middle of it that showed its insides was made out of streaks of white and brown.

"The judge put it all together, Little Charlie. He said it was misfortune and bad luck on a unimaginable scale. This here stone was imbedded in that maple. Wasn't no way to tell by looking at the tree, but when Big Charlie struck that first blow, this was right under the bark."

"How's a stone gonna get under the bark of a tree, sir, 'specially one that big?"

"Near's the judge figgered, this stone sat in the tree for forty-two year, three month, and four or so days. You's too young to remember, but that's how long ago the Tornado of Eighteen Hunnert and Sixteen come through and jus' 'bout blowed Possum Moan and most of the Tanner plantation right off the map."

Grandpap use to tell stories 'bout what they called the Big Blow. Said so many crops was blowed away that lots of sharecroppers starved and even the Tanners got sunk so low they had to sell off some slaves.

Sheriff Jackson said, "The old folks what seent it say God took a notion to scratch his forefinger along the earth, meddling with humans jus' for a laugh. But didn't no one find it funny. We lost nineteen souls and the Tanners had thirty-six darkies kilt on one day.

"There was whole passels of folks what weren't never the same afterward. If the chance come up, go sneak a look at the backs of Alda Santos's hands and arms. She wasn't but four when it happened and there's still dirt that got blowed into her so hard that it went under her skin and ain't coming out till the worms chaw through and reclaim it."

I wasn't 'bout to sneak no looks at Miss Daponte; 'twas well knowed that 'long with being the strongest woman in Possum Moan, she was also the orneriest one.

The sheriff said, "Same thing occurred with this here stone. We figgered it got blowed into that maple when the tree was young, got itself stuck and's been sitting there for near half a cent'ry. Sat there so long that as the tree growed, the bark crawled right o'er top it."

So that 'splains it.

That's a perfect sample of the luck of the Bobos; a million and nine trees out there in 'em woods and Pap had to go pick the only one that was toting a invisible shield.

The sheriff shook his head.

"Strong's your daddy was, when he laid into that maple, the head of the ax must've hit the stone, which caused 'em sparks you seent, then it ricocheted back like a bat shot outta the bad place.

"I guess the history books has got to be rewrit; it's took forty-two year, three month, and a day or two for the Finger of God to steal its twentieth soul."

I heard a long slow breath come outta me.

The sheriff hummed and hawed 'round as though he had more to say. Finally he jus' bust out with, "You got to understand your size is confusing to folk, Little Charlie. Your pa looked like two full-growed men joined into one, and you look like a man and a half. It's easy to forget you ain't nothing but a boy. And a good boy too.

"I'm truly 'shamed that I wasn't more considerate of you at this time of your mourning. I 'pologize for all I put you through. I hopes you can 'cept my 'pology."

"Yes, sir, I do. Pap always says you's a good man."

The sheriff handed me the stone.

"We gouged this out the tree and thought you might want to keep it."

I didn't know what to say. I wasn't gonna be rude and look no gift horse in the mouth, but I didn't know what the sheriff 'spected me to do with a stone that had took part in killing my pap.

I guess me and Ma *could* drive a couple of nails into the cabin walls and set the stone on 'em. That way if anyone ever come to call on us, we could say, "Bet you a dollar you can't guess what this here stone done."

And we'd win the dollar every time.

Then the sheriff picked up the burlap sack and pult out something flat and shiny.

It took me a second to see 'twas Pap's ax-head. The striking edge had folded back on itself.

"Folks knew your pa was a powerful man, Little Charlie, but didn't no one know jus' how powerful. We fount this ten feet off the ground wedged in a oak. We wiped the blood off and figgered it's yourn too."

All I could say was, "Me and Ma gives our thanks to you and the posse for the trouble y'all went through to get these, Sheriff Jackson."

I put the stone under my right arm and helt the ax-head in my left hand. I give the sheriff a handshake and went back inside.

Soon's I opened the door, Ma got more 'thusiastic with the loudness of her snoring.

I turned the ax-head o'er and o'er, wondering what to do with it. Best I could come up with would be to hang it right next to where I was gonna hang the flat stone.

That way if a caller ever did come, I could raise the bet up and make me two dollars.

CHAPTER 5

The Apocky-Lips Come A-Knocking

Sheriff Jackson must have the gift of prophesizing, 'cause I'll be blanged if the days after Pa's burying didn't see me and Ma get two bowls of tater salad and four new horseshoes for Spangler.

Then no visitors or nothing in the days after.

That's one the reasons I was so surprised when early one morning afore we headed out for the fields, there was a pounding on the door like we'd stole food from someone.

A door getting banged on hard makes you jump right up and answer, even if you don't want to.

I opened the door and looked down at the man who'd been a-knocking. It took me a second to rec-a-nize him and when I did, all my breathing and thinking come dead to a stop.

The last time I seent this man was a year ago when he was clenching on to a blood-dripping whip whilst standing o'er the shredded-open back of Mr. Tom Foster, the poor farmer that works the plots next to ourn.

I would've knowed who this was right off 'cept now that I's seeing him up close, he wasn't nothing but a scrap of a person, not much taller than Ma. He always 'peared to be gigantic when he was tearing strips offen someone's back or barking orders from atop his horse or when he was getting whispered 'bout in folks' gossip. His legs was so bowed that most of his tallness was going sideways 'stead of up.

Me and the man both looked at one the 'nother in surprise. I couldn't move a finger whilst Cap'n Buck, the Tanners' o'erseer, eyed me head to toe, like he's sizing up a horse he was 'bout to buy.

Everyone say the man is not to be messed with, so I showed my best manners.

"Morning, Cap'n, sir. Something the matter?"

He looked up at me and said, "By Gawd! If you ain't the spit and image of your pa. Same pale skin, same sandy-brown hair, and same puke-green eyes. They tolt me you was huge but I didn't have no idea. How old is you?"

"I'm jus' 'bout to turn thirteen, sir. Is something wrong?"

"Oh, nothing that caint be fixed. Where's your ma at?"

"She ain't up to no visitors, sir. My pap died not long ago."

"I heard. Don't much go on 'round here that get past me, but for the past two weeks, I been engaged in bringing a couple of coffles back from the markets in Charleston. That's why it took me so long to find out Big Charlie Bobo done kilt hisself. I come soon's I heard. I needs to see your ma."

"I'm sorry, sir, but she ain't taking no visitors yet. I'll pass your good wishes on to her."

The cap'n snorted. "Oh, really? I'll tell you what, I'll pass 'em myself. Where she at?"

I wondered what Pap would do, but it wouldn't-a happened to Pap; the cap'n wouldn't never come a-banging on our door if Pap was here.

I musta outweighed him by near eighty pounds; if I punched him right on top of that big head of his, I knowed he'd be out for the count.

But I had other things to think on. This

man had a rep-a-tation knowed even beyond Richland District. Some say he's knowed 'bout all 'crost the state.

One day last December, Pap come home in a turrible state after he spent a afternoon working on the Tanner plantation. We'd needed supplies bad and was out of credit at the store and hadn't had near nothing to eat in days, so Pap had axed Miss Tanner for some work. He'd tolt her he'd even help in the field with the slaves.

She said she'd never have no white man working next to slaves but that Pap should go see the cap'n and have him give Pap some things to do. She even give him some old fatback they was gonna give their slaves.

When Pap got home, he looked turrible. He give Ma the pork and tolt her he wouldn't be eating 'cause he seent things that had ruint his appetite.

He'd said, "That blackheart Cap'n Buck, someone who does 'em things for reasons other than duty, ain't got no soul. I won't never go back there, I don't care if we gots to eat rocks; nothing's worth having to see what I jus' seent. Nothing."

Pap had said something 'bout cat-hauling and I interrupted and axed what that was.

Ma tolt Pap to hesh up.

No matter how much I begged 'em, Pap

nor Ma never would tell me what sort of things Cap'n Buck had did. Nor what goes on when cats is getting hauled.

"Growed folks' business" was all they'd say, and I knowed that meant to let the whole thing be.

But it wasn't nowhere near that easy for Pap to be quit of it. Not only didn't he eat for a couple of days, it was weeks afore he slept through a whole night without terrorfying me and Ma by waking up screaming and begging someone to stop. 'Twas as if this cat-hauling had got done to Pap hisself 'stead of someone else.

The mystery of all 'em things going through my mind chased away any thinking 'bout taking a poke at the cap'n's head.

"But, sir, it don't make no sense talking to Ma; she ain't in her right head."

He looked up at me and the feeling that he was fixing to do something rough jumped offen him.

I could feel myself blushing and tensing up to fight back.

He said, "I ain't one to repeat myself less'n I'm dealing with someone what's deef or someone what's dumb as a bucket of rocks, boy. And since you's hearing everything I say clear's a bell, you's clearly a member of the second group. So for the third and last time, I'm axing, where she at?"

He didn't wait for a answer. I stood aside as he come into the house. He didn't even pull off his hat.

A most peculiar smell that set my eyes a-stinging followed behind him.

He went o'er and, without as much as a "Howdy do," pult aside the sheet that divides the cabin in two at night.

"Morning, Miss Bobo."

Ma had the cover o'er most her head, only a knob of gray-and-brown hair was poking out at the top. But the way her hands was gripping tight on the covers and shaking give 'way that she was only pretending to sleep.

The cap'n sat at the foot of Pap and Ma's bed and said, "I'm sure sorrowed to hear 'bout Big Charlie's run-in with that ax. I was shocked when I heard, but I'm telling you the whole thing is a sign."

Ma pulled the covers down and cleared her throat.

"Oh! Cap'n Buck. A sign, you said, sir?"

"Oh, yes, I ain't certain of the chapter nor the verse, but I knows somewhere in the Bible it say something 'long the lines of 'When the trees starts to fighting back 'gainst the woodsman, it's a definite sign that the end is near and that the apocky-lips is nigh upon us.' "

He put his hand next to his ear and said, "Yes, ma'am, Miss Bobo, if you listen careful, you can hear it. Does y'all hear the knocking?"

Me and Ma, not hearing nothing, 'changed a quick worried look.

The cap'n said, "Be that as it may, that ain't why I'm calling. Me and Big Charlie has some unfinished business that needs tending to right away."

The cap'n's knowed to be mad as a hatter, but even someone crazy as him had to know all Pap's business here on earth is through.

Ma was looking jus' as confused as me. She said, "Business, sir?"

"Yes, ma'am. 'Bout a month ago, me and Big Charlie made some plans to go north. All I was waiting on was getting the word to go.

"Well, wouldn't you know it, the word come jus' 'bout two weeks ago whilst I was in Charleston. So now I lost me a week and a half and time's pressing on me hard. You ain't got no idea how disappointed I'm feeling now that Big Charlie won't be coming north with me."

"He never said nothing to me 'bout going

north, sir. And of course now . . ."

"Well, ma'am, Big Charlie tolt me the only way he could go was if I paid him half his wages 'fore going and half once we got back.

"I tolt him he'd lost his mind, but, as it does so often, my kind and generous nature overpowered my common sense and I give him one-tenth of his share up front. And now, unfair as it may be, I'm left to rouse up someone else to travel with and ain't got the time to do it proper.

"All that said, I'll respectfully leave you and your boy to your mourning soon's y'all scramble 'round and fetch me the fifty dollars I give your husband."

The walls of the cabin started crowding me.

Ma was horrified. She sat bolt upright and whispered, "Fifty dollars! Sir, I can assure you Charlie ain't never come home with that kind of money. Nothing close to no fifty dollars! Why, you's free to look through the house if you wants, but we ain't never had the such in here.

"*Fifty dollars?* Other than Mr. Tanner, I don't even know no one that's ever had fifty dollars at one time, sir. My hand to Jesus."

The cap'n closed his eyes for a couple seconds, opened 'em, then smiled. Leastways, I think it was a smile; the cap'n's moustache was growed so wild that it hung o'er his lips like thick Spanish moss in a swamp. But a crinkling come to his eyes, and with most folks, that's a sign that they's smiling.

"You know what, Miss Bobo, I gots a good sense 'bout these things and I can see you's being truthful. I believe you when you say Big Charlie never gave y'all no money."

Me and Ma both untensed ourselves.

But done it too soon.

The cap'n said, "Yes, ma'am, I sure 'nough think that's the truth.

"But that ain't got one chicken-scratching thing to do with my fifty dollars. From what I can tell, Big Charlie ain't got no plans on paying it back, so as his heirs, it ain't nothing but common sense that that job's fell to y'all."

"Cap'n Buck, how —"

He helt up his hand.

"Now, ain't nothing I'd rather do more'n chat the hours away with y'all; we could tell stories 'bout Big Charlie Bobo for days, but I'm pressed for time. Either you or that freak-show-size boy of yourn go get my money."

He pulled a pocket watch out his jacket, tapped it, and said, "Time's a-wasting."

"But, sir, you can't be serious. Look at us,

we ain't got nothing. We's barely eating."

"Big Charlie don't own this land no more, do he?"

"No, sir, not for going on six years. Things got squeezish on us, so he sold it to Mr. Tanner's boy; we jus' sharecropping now."

The cap'n walked to the door and called o'er his shoulder, "I got to ride down to Orangeburg District and see if Scooch Stinson can come 'long north with me. I'll be back first thing tomorrow. So, for the next twenty-four hours, let's all set to figgering out how y'all's gonna come up with my money."

Ma was sobbing. "But, sir, there jus' ain't . . ."

But Cap'n Buck was gone.

Me and Ma didn't even have to say nothing to each other.

We was of one mind.

The only thing I was worried 'bout was Stanky being out on her morning run through the woods.

I hoped she'd get back afore we left.

CHAPTER 6

Bit, Chawed On, Swallowed, and Spit Back Out

We give the cap'n a hour to make sure he wasn't gonna double back, then I hitched Spangler to the wagon and pult it from behind the shed. We started loading up our goods.

Truth tolt, it was me who started loading up our goods. Ma wasn't much help at all. She was so scairt of the cap'n that she was jumping at every owl hoot and near tackling me whenever something rustled 'gainst a branch in the woods out back. I kept hoping it would be Stanky making one 'em rustles, but she never showed.

To give Ma a little com-fitting, I went to the shed and reached under the floorboards to get Pap's pistol. I put the last six shells from the box in it.

I made Ma set on the buckboard seat and

tolt her to keep a eye out with the pistol in her lap.

"Jus' make sure you don't shoot Stanky."

It's a stretch to call where we lives a cabin. Most folk that know us calls it the Bobo shack, so I never would've thought we had much in it. But once I finished packing our few pieces of furniture and our clothes and Pap's tools from the shed and the almost finished cabinet of Mr. Dalton's, the small buckboard was so chock-full that things was hanging o'er the sides.

Daybreak was still probably a hour away when I finally got everything tied proper to the wagon. I clumb up and sat next to Ma.

I called and whistled one last time for Stanky.

Ma spit o'er the side and said, "Good riddance. This place wasn't nothing but trouble from day one. Where we gonna go, Charlie?"

I said, "First we's got to go east to Sumter District, then we'll go north through Kershaw. Cap'n Buck said he was heading to Orangeburg District, which ain't but fifteen miles south of here. I don't wanna go direct north in case he come after us. It'd be something turrible if we was to run into him on the road."

Ma's eyes was wild. "Charlie, you listen to

me and you listen good. If you ever see that man again, I don't care if it five year from now, you gotta swear you'll wait your chance and empty this pistol on him.

"It don't matter if you shoots him from behind, you gotta do it. He was right, you know, your pa's dying that way is a sign that the world's coming to a end. And that man would know too; he's the devil's messenger.

"I wouldn't let your pa tell you 'bout the things the cap'n done to Mr. Tanner's slaves, but believe me, that man ain't human.

"I ain't one to think darkies should be getting no special treatment, things is too soft on 'em as is. I heard most of 'em lives better than good hardworking white folk. But what your pa tolt me the cap'n done to chirren to get back at they ma and pa sets me shivering jus' thinking 'bout it.

"Cat-hauling a two-year-old 'cause her ma skipped off the plantation for a couple hour? I don't know how low someone got to be sunk to think up doing something that evil.

"Whatever happen, we can't let him get holt of us. Promise me you . . ."

There time goes again, being a trickster and having things that was happening reg'lar pace slow down jus' 'nough so's I was gonna be forced to watch every turrible drawed-out second.

I ain't sure if it was the way Ma's face twisted so's she had the same look that Grandma did the day she died, or if the highness of her shriek was what made me draw up and cringe.

She fumbled in her lap and come up gripping the pistol with both hands. She couldn't even wait to get it all the way unwrapped from the curtains of George Washington's cousin.

The first explosion had me ducking and covering my head.

I looked o'er my shoulder to see what had scairt Ma so bad.

Sure 'nough, there, sitting astride his horse not ten yards from us, was Cap'n Buck, his eyes crinkling up in a horrible smile!

My and his eyes both got pult back to Ma and the pistol; it looked five times bigger in her hands than it did when Pap helt it. Ma's first shot had blowed a hole in the piece of curtain and one of the gold tassels had busted out afire.

The second shot belched out the barrel with a ball of sparks and a flame that lit up the front of the wagon. It was a good thing Ma was gripping on to it with both hands;

66

the recoil sent the gun jumping o'er her head.

The third and fourth shots happened so quick one after the 'nother that Ma didn't have no chance to level the gun at the cap'n. Two bullets screamed off into the early morning sky.

Pap must not've give Ma the same shooting lessons he give me. Or maybe he did and she forgot 'em. She was doing everything he'd said not to. She was taking raggedy fast-fast breaths and 'stead of thinking 'bout where each shot was aimed, she quit thinking 'bout anything but getting as many of them bullets out that pistol quick as she could.

The fifth shot whizzed by me, then thumped into a tree di-rect behind the cap'n.

The sixth shot grazed my pants leg gentle as a kitten rubbing itself 'gainst my shin.

When Ma finally rasseled the curtain most the way off and got the gun level, it was too late. She was plumb outta bullets and the click-click-click of the dry-firing pistol echoed 'gainst the trees 'round the cabin. Them turrible clicks sounded just as loud to me as the six rounds she'd fired.

Shooting that pistol wore Ma right out; when she brung it down she looked more beat than she would working the fields from sunup to sundown on a hot July day.

Me, Ma, and Cap'n Buck sat there froze.

I'd swear we helt on to that pose for a hour. The cap'n was the first to say something.

"My, my, my," he chuckled. "If the way the Bobos traditionally say good morning to a visitor is by firing six shots at him, I'm letting one and all know, this here's my last time a-calling!

"And look, y'all never said nothing 'bout going off. Why, if I'd-a knowed, I would've stayed here and helped pack the wagon."

It's hard to know what to say to someone right after your ma's took six shots at him from point-blank range. After that, no 'mount of 'pologizing is gonna get took to heart, so I figgered it'd be best to change the subject.

I said, "No, sir, that's kind of you, but we don't need no help. We's heading o'er to Auntie May-May's jus' up the road for a week or two to try and get Ma better. She been feeling puny lately and —"

The cap'n chuckled and said, "You want to know why I'm so good at my job, big man?"

Them last two words sounded as though he was cussing me.

"You ever heard of having something called the sixth sense?"

I stared at him.

"Well, I've been blessed with what's knowed as the seventh sense. I gets these inklings when someone's plotting 'gainst me, this kind of itching in my skin when plans is getting laid to do me or mine wrong.

"And I gotta tell you, boy, the minute I left you and your ma, my skin took to creeping and crawling like I'd pitched tent on a nest of ants! I tried fighting the feeling and says to myself, 'Naw, Cap, them Bobos is good folks, they ain't up to nothing.'

"And I ain't got no problem unnastanding how losing your husband and pa so tragic might get y'all feeling a bit unsociable, but six shots to the face? Maybe it's jus' me, but that do seem to go right past being unfriendly; that go all the way to being downright hos-tile.

"Why, I'm getting the feeling y'all ain't glad to see the ol' cap'n. Please tell me I'm wrong."

I'd seent this afore. I'd seent this when a barn cat gets holt of a mouse and bites something on it hard 'nough that the mouse can't run proper no more. And all that happens for the next hour, or however long the cat's having fun, is the mouse gets batted 'round and bit at and chawed on and licked and swallowed and spit back out till this pitiful look come to its eyes and it's so scairt and wore out that its heart leap right out its chest.

Can't be no worst way to die.

I wasn't 'bout to play this game with the cap'n.

He said, "I decided to lay o'er there till the itching passed. And since I jus' got off the road, I couldn't help myself. I falls fast to sleep. And it's a good thing for both of us I did; I woke up jus' in time to help y'all on your journey."

His voice changed and he said to Ma, "Gal, do you got any idea the pickle you done put us all in? What's this gonna do to my rep-a-tation once folks fount out what you jus' done?

"I spent all these years getting these hicks and darkies to know me real good and to see real clear where the lines is drawed. I keeps things simple. When word of this gets out, it ain't gonna do nothing but serve to confuse 'em.

"I can see them yokels debating with one the 'nother 'bout what was the 'mount of shots they could take at the ol' cap'n without suffering no repa-cussions.

"They'll be scratching their heads and saying nonsense such as, 'Is it OK to take seven shots at him or is the limit six?'

"Or they'll whisper to one another, 'Mebbe the ol' cap'n won't mind if we was to empty *two* pistols on him, he's turnt into being a right reasonable man.'

"And imagine how befuddled them darkies is gonna be when it come to using a double-barrel shotgun. They gonna have the worstest of times trying to figger if they's allowed to reload three times or six.

"Why, I'd get exhausted and be a nervous wreck dodging bullets from sunup to sundown. And you tell me, how many nervous, jumpy men you got respect for?

"Plus" — he wiped away at a pretend tear — "I gotta say, you gone and hurt my feelings, Miss Bobo.

"How's I s'pose to let you live after you done sullied my rep-a-tation so?"

Ma didn't know she was part of a cat-and-mouse show; she was happy to play 'long. It was right pitiful the way she set to begging.

"Oh, please, Mr. Cap'n Buck, sir. I ain't gonna breathe a word 'bout none of this, and neither will Charlie. I swear, sir. Tell him. Tell the man you won't say nothing. Charlie Bobo! Wipe that look off your face and *tell him*!"

I wish Ma would jus' close her mouth.

The sooner she was quiet, the sooner this toying with us would be o'er.

"How foolish I look, gal? You might not want to say nothing, but it's been my 'sperience that words has a way of spouting out of stupid folk the same way water spouts out a spring, it jus' happen. My rep-a-tation saves me a whole lot of trouble and grief and you gone and kicked a hole in it that I ain't got no choice but to plug up."

"I swear, Cap'n Buck, I swear we won't say nothing. Please give us a chance."

The cap'n wasn't through toying with Ma. "Afore I bring this to a end, Miss Bobo, why don't you tell me what y'all's heard 'bout me."

Ma was fumbling 'round, trying to think of what answer he wanted to hear.

She said, "All I heard, Cap'n Buck, is you's a great and powerful man, sir. They all say you's the real reason Mr. Tanner's rich as he is."

"Go on."

I was sick of this game.

I yelled at him, "They all say you's the sickest, most vile piece of garbage on this earth. They say your ma was a skunk and your pa was a rat. They say there's a special spot in the bad place a-waiting the day you gets what you deserves. That's what they say, you stanking piece of human filth."

Ma throwed herself in the dirt off the wagon, moaning, 'lowing Pap's pistol to fall into the dust.

I didn't care. Her taking 'em six shots at him and missing was the end of the road for the two of us. I could see the direction this whole thing was headed for and knowed, begging or not, it wasn't gonna be but a minute or two afore the cap'n got tired of toying with us. I knowed in my heart that Little Charlie Bobo and Suzie Bobo was gonna be the next names on the list of folks he'd sent to the graveyard.

We was already dead and I wasn't gonna spend my last minutes on earth begging no worm from the bottom of a outhouse for my life.

My pap never would've and neither would I.

The cap'n needed to do what he needed to do and get it o'er with.

He smiled and said, "You right, boy. That's 'zactly what they be saying 'bout me, and ooh, Your Honor, I'm guilty of every charge!"

I couldn't take no more. Something turrible was 'bout to happen to Ma, but that didn't mean I had to be 'round to see it.

I jumped off the wagon and rushed the

cap'n's horse with nothing but a balled-up fist and, 'shamed as it make me, tears running down my face.

With one quick move a six-shooter was in his hand.

He knowed what I was thinking. 'Stead of plugging me, he draws a bead on Ma, who was worming 'round in the dirt, still begging and crying.

"You ever seent what someone who been gutshot go through 'fore they die? Take one more step and your ma will show how it's done."

I didn't want to, but I froze.

He tolt Ma, "The only reason I ain't put you down is 'cause if I was to give you your jus' deserts, this boy would hate me so much that he wouldn't be no good to me.

"I likes what I jus' seent from him. The boy got heart; I'm in a bad pinch and it seem the good Lord done answered my prayers and sent your boy to fulfill my needs. Besides, time ain't on my side. So I'm gonna be a good businessman and a good Christian and forgive your transgressions and hope y'all'll forgive mine.

"Here's what's 'bout to happen. Woman, you gonna run on down to the Foster place and tell Tom I needs him to bring a horse to hitch to this here wagon. Then he's to pull it o'er to barn number three on the Tanner north sixty. You unna-stand me?"

Ma was trembling something fierce, but she said, "Yes, sir, oh, thank you, sir, you's the saint folks say you is. It was Jesus hisself what was protecting you from them bullets! Hallelujah!"

The cap'n said, "Is you paying 'tention, gal? What barn do I want him to take my wagon to?"

"Barn number three on the Tanner north sixty, sir."

"Y'all's lost possession of the wagon and everything in it. That's the first payment on your debt."

He turned to me.

"Ain't that horse from Joe Sell's mare?"

I didn't say nothing.

Ma piped in. "Yes, sir! Big Charlie bought Spangler back when we was flush, paid near a hunnert dollars for him. Take him! He's a great one!"

"That's what I remembered, sired by . . ."

Ma said, "He was sired by Grand Shavois!"

The cap'n said, "He'll do."

He turned to me. "You gonna unhitch that horse and saddle him up. I ain't got time to see if Scooch Stinson can come north, and since the Bobo I already paid went and kilt his fool self, you's vola-teering to take his place."

He didn't have no call at all to say Pap was a fool. None.

"You's bigger than most full-growed men. If you keep your hat pulled low and your mouth shut, all I really need is someone to bluff folks and gimme another set of eyes to make sure don't nothing go wrong behind my back."

He said to Ma, "Me and your boy gonna be back in three, four weeks, a month and a half at the most."

I said, "A month and a half? But I can't leave the crops, it's jus' 'bout time for us to —"

The cap'n helt up his hand. "You got bigger fish to fry now; besides, the sheriff was coming out here next week to kick y'all off the land anyhow. We figgered with Big Charlie gone, wasn't no way y'all could keep it up. We'll send some darkies o'er to bring y'all's crops in.

"You and me gonna run us down some thieves. Ten years ago, they stole jus' 'bout four thousand dollars from Mr. Tanner. It took that long for word to get back where they's at.

"They set up house in Dee-troit, Mitch-again. Ten years has gone by and they up there thinking they got 'way with it; they let theyselves get careless.

"But they 'bout to get a big surprise; justice sleeps but not for long and one day when it wake up, all sins is atoned for."

"But, Cap'n Buck —"

He yells, "Boy, do you know how much Jesus has graced you with His love on this day? You and your ma was fixing to steal fifty dollars from me, she done took six cracks at blowing my head off, and y'all ain't said one true thing to me since we met. Even Job would've got so vexed with y'all that he'd've personally smashed y'all's heads in for any one of them things.

"But 'stead of harming y'all, I'm letting your ma go free and offering you a chance to make the easiest fifty dollars you'll ever make in your life. Plus, I'm-a give you another fifty once we get them thieves back here. And 'stead of getting down on your knees and licking my boots, you gonna whine and gimme some 'But, Cap'n Bucks'?"

Ma screams, "You shet up, Charlie! You shet your fool mouth! Jus' ride on 'long with the cap'n and don't be sassing the man neither. He doing us a big favor. You hurry 'long and don't be no trouble to him. Your pa owe the man fifty dollars and it's on you

77

to honor the debt. You been raised proper and best show the cap'n what a gennel-man you is."

The cap'n's eyes rolled.

He said, "What you gonna do, boy? How smart is you? Is we gonna settle this right on the spot" — he took the pistol off of Ma and put it on me — "or is you gonna take advantage of this chance I'm giving you? Is you gonna re-deem your pa's good name?"

Ma yells, "He gonna do it, Cap'n, and with your permission, sir, I'm already on my way to get Mr. Foster."

She rose out the dirt, pulled up her shift, and started running barefoot down the road toward the Foster farm.

The cap'n said, "Reach me that pistol, boy."

I handed him Pap's pistol. My hands was shaking hard.

He put it in one of his saddlebags.

"Now go on and do what I said."

My legs and hands was trembling some-thing turrible whilst I unhitched Spangler, saddled him up, and clumb on his back.

Me and the cap'n started on the road north.

We hadn't rode but a couple of miles when the cap'n pulled his horse up.

"I ain't saying I don't trust your ma, but

seeing what she done, having a doubt or two 'bout her intentions seems justified. You wait here. I'm gonna go back and make sure your ma ain't plotting to get my wagon pulled somewhere else."

He turned back down the road, calling o'er his shoulder, "Don't do nothing stupid, Little Charlie Bobo. If you ain't here when I get back, ooh-ooh-ooh-wee!"

There ain't no way of knowing how long I sat there atop Spangler afore my mind started clearing from being scairt near to death.

The first thing that come to me was the turrible danger the cap'n riding back alone was putting Ma in. Maybe he changed his mind, maybe he figgered he had to kill her. But if that was true, how come he made such a fuss 'bout where he wanted our wagon to be took to?

As I's sitting there trying to figger what to do, my ears got keen to every sound in the forest, to the birds and the crickets, to the wind in the trees and the toady-frogs and whatever it was that was rooting 'round behind 'em trees.

The sound my ears was dreading they was gonna hear most was a scream. Or a gun-shot.

Questions started chawing 'way at me.

Should I ride back and try to stop him afore he done anything harsh to Ma? Should I ride off to Possum Moan to get the sheriff for help? Should I find some way to bushwhack the cap'n?

When I finished thinking on it, I knowed I didn't have no choice but to go find Ma. I was jus' 'bout to turn Spangler back down the road when something I heard made my insides melt and run down in my stomach.

I couldn't help it, I leant o'er Spangler's side and retched. I hadn't had nothing to eat since midday yesterday, so it was mostly water that come out.

A horse was clomping slow up the road and whoever was riding it was singing.

The cap'n.

He was singing in a scratchy, chills-making voice that coulda come right up from the bad place.

. . . the darkies roll on the little cabin floor,
All merry, all happy and bright:
By 'n' by Hard Times comes a knocking at
    the door,
Then my old Kentucky Home, good night!

When he rode up next to me, he was smiling and his eyes was aglow.

He said, "I never should've doubted her;

she was well down the road to Tom Foster's. She's quite the runner, your ma. Reminded me of a doe as she bounded through the forest. A good woman that. Last thing she tolt me was 'Oh, thank you for being so kind to us, Cap'n, thank you so much.'"

That was 'zactly the kind of corn Ma would dish out. Relief come o'er me so much I near fainted out the saddle.

"Thank you, Cap'n Buck, sir. My ma is right, Pap would've wanted me to honor his debt. I ain't gonna be no trouble to you."

He put the spurs to his horse and said, "We needs to get moving, boy. And if you change your mind and gives me one moment of grief, I will kill you, come back and kill your ma and anything else that was ever alive on that land."

"No, sir, no need for that, a Bobo's word is his bond."

We was headed north . . . but my heart was somewhere out in 'em woods with Stanky.

❧ CHAPTER 7 ❧

The Education of Little Charlie Bobo

The good thing 'bout trailing 'long behind the cap'n is that I wasn't likely to see nothing that was gonna bring Pap to mind. After his accident, everything 'round our cabin or out in the fields pointed back to him.

I couldn't walk by the shed without 'membering that it was here that me and him had done this or that together, or that it was o'er there that he'd cuffed me for being hard-headed, or that it was everywhere and always that I was a second away from hearing his rumblin' voice calling out, "Little Charlie, you know that ain't the best you could do . . ." or "Now, son, your ma don't mean nothing by . . ." or "That's my boy . . ."

Plodding 'long behind the cap'n was keeping all 'em worries and thoughts at bay, but it was also giving me a 'preciation for me and Ma's talk 'bout working in the fields.

Ma has a peculiar way of looking at most things, but every once in the while she makes sense. And the more days that passed and the more north we got, seemed like Ma's idea 'bout bumbly bees and ants wasn't as much a waste of time as I thought at first.

She'd tolt me, "Jus' 'cause God give you a brain don't mean you gots to show off and use it to poke at and worry 'bout everything you see every day, do it? That ain't nothing but a gay-run-teed way to wear your brain out or get it so tired that when times come and you really do need to use it, it ain't gonna want to get up and go. You s'posed to be smart, Charlie; that brain of yourn only got so much in it; you keep going to it as though it's a well and dipping water out, mark my words, one day it gonna run dry and leave you mad as a March hare.

"If you was really smart as you think you is, you'd quit looking for answers inside your own head and start looking for 'em in God's gifts.

"You needs to be more like a bumbly bee, Charlie. Ain't you never seent how them bees'll burrow theyself into so many flowers that they very color change? They go from being yellow and black and common-looking to wearing balls of gold all o'er every square inch of theyselves. And there ain't no mistaking neither that once them bees is wearing those robes of gold, they's close to Jesus as they can get, they's happy as anything living can be. They'll sit on the edge of that flower just soaking it all in afore they starts buzzing their wings and celebrating that sound they makes. That's where you needs to be if you gonna learn how to work these fields; you need to quit thinking so much and listen to that buzz. You need to give that brain of yourn a break so's it will be there when you really do need it."

Following behind the cap'n, I tried for the longest time doing it Ma's way and trying to hear nothing but the bees buzzing, but it was 'gainst my nature; it wasn't the type of thing that set easy with me. I couldn't help but wondering where one trail led off to or what the name of the town we was drifting by was. I'd-a drove myself crazy if I kept thinking 'bout a dusty, pollen-covered bee smiling on his way back to the hive.

'Cepting for the horses' hoofs clomping on the hard dirt, and the every-once-in-the-while farts that was drifting back from either the cap'n or his horse, the first couple of days of us heading north was mostly quiet.

Deadly quiet.

So quiet that I didn't want to do nothing more than scream so harsh that my throat would get raggedy.

But one of the first things the cap'n let me know was that he didn't want to hear no talking or sounds from me until he was sure I was smart 'nough to be worthwhile to listen to.

Which left me wondering how he could figger if I was worthwhile to listen to if I wasn't 'lowed to do no talking.

It only took him a day and a half to figger out that *I* should listen to everything he had to say to me.

Maybe being alone most the time and having folk scairt and hateful toward you would make anyone lonely and this was the cap'n's only chance to get some reg'lar talking done.

Whilst he was talking, it would've been real simple to hear the bees and fall 'sleep but I 'membered something Pap had said once. I ain't sure of the 'zact words but the nut of it was, "You can learn from anybody. Even dimwits can teach you if you listen careful and pick out the kernels of corn from the horse crap they's dishing out."

The cap'n said we was probably out of South Carol-liney and into North Carol-liney and the words started pouring out of him.

It didn't take many miles to see his favorite thing to talk about was how smart he was and how he was better'n anybody else.

"This here's the finest job you gonna find," he said. "This a job that ain't never gonna go nowhere, it ain't never gonna change. 'Cause of this job, I ain't got nothing in common with y'all sharecroppers and dirt farmers who's got to depend on the whims of weather or weevils or whether or not you got a decent crew of darkies with a good white man who know how to work 'em. Uh-uh, I ain't got to worry 'bout none of that.

"This job don't depend on nothing but the nature of them darkies and the laws of this land and them's two things that ain't never gonna change. You gots two hunnert years of history that proves it. Sure as the sun rise in the east, it's a fac' of life.

"My pa and his pa afore him and his pa afore him and his pa afore that was overseers for the Tanners. And if the good Lord would've seent fit to gimme a child, he'd've been one too.

"Way I see it, jus' as long as 'em Tanners keeps pumping out a healthy baby or two every generation, and don't have another long run of mo-rons, I'm in high cotton."

He reached into his pocket and pult something round and bronzy out.

He said, "You see this? You know what it is?"

I reached to take it out his hand. He pult it back.

"I didn't say nothing 'bout you touching it; I said look."

It was a badge of some kind with a big star in the middle and letters circling all the way 'round the outside edge.

"What is it?"

"Can't you read, boy?"

"Some words, but not them ones."

"It say I'm a official South Carol-liney slave catcher. Best job God created."

Then he got onto his second favorite thing to bump his gums about: slaves and what horrible beasts they is.

"Them darkies is the most ungrateful animals you's ever gonna come 'cross. No matter how good they gets treated, no matter how much you give 'em, it ain't 'nough. You caint satisfy 'em, and you's a fool if you try.

"They's always looking to get something more, and iffen they gets it or iffen they don't, sooner or later their nature starts a-boiling and they gonna be unhappy and want to run. It's in their blood. They ain't nothing but chirren and they ain't gonna never be nothing but chirren.

"And don't matter what you do, their nature ain't changing. Two hunnert years has showed you can't beat it out of 'em, you can't bleed it out of 'em, you can't breed it out of 'em. Two hunnert years of trying and here we is in the year of our Lord eighteen hunnert and fifty-eight and I still gotta waste my time doing the same old nonsense my great-great-grandpaps done.

"Which is all pretty good evy-dence that overseeing's here to stay.

"Only other folks that got this reg'lar a job is the darkies theyselfs. And that's jus' one more thing they ain't got no 'preciation for."

It was getting near dark when the cap'n said, "We'll pull up here."

We was at a spot where a campfire was burning and there was five or six other men gathered 'round.

The people tolt us we was welcome to stay with 'em.

There was one old man who looked like he was friendly.

We introduced ourselves and he said to the cap'n, "You ain't got to tell me what y'all do."

He pointed at the cap'n. "Not you any-way."

He pointed at me next. "Now that I looks at you up close, I see you ain't nothing but a kid jus' outta diapers."

It was dark but the blushing come on strong.

The man winked at me and said, "Come sit next to me, boy."

I looked at the cap'n, he nodded his head and tolt the friendly man, "You so good at guessing what folk do, what's your line of work?"

"I spent half my life sailing and the other half working the rails. Before, between, and since, I done everything else. Ain't a job you can name I ain't done."

He looked at the cap'n. "I stands corrected. I ain't never had nothing to do with slaving."

The cap'n snorted.

One of the other men said, "Ol' Jerry here was telling us 'bout why he give up being a cap'n on a ship and switched o'er to working the rails."

Ol' Jerry said, "The main reason I give up being a sailor was they got this one ridic-a-lus rule that the crew's got to be the last boodle of folk to get off once the ship start sinking. And what's worst is the cap'n's suppose to be the last one off.

"I don't know and it ain't none my concern whether or not y'all's religious men, but *my* Bible clearly state that you can't go 'round killing yourself. Suicide's plainly a sin. And being the last one off a ship is suicide if you's to ask me.

"I knowed if push come to shove and the boat was going down and the lifeboats was full but for one seat and there was a frail old Virginny lady or some young 'un looking to take it, it would sound a powerful lot like suicide to me if I didn't get involved in some type of tussling for that last seat.

"So, to make sure there wasn't gonna be no moral di-lemma, I jumped ship and took up being a railroad man. I soon fount out railroad folk was a lot more reasonable when it come to who gets saved and who don't.

"Lemme give you some proof.

"There was this old bridge jus' outside Hamburg, South Carol-liney, that everyone knowed was only a matter of time 'fore it went down. Every crew that crossed her tolt the company over and over that it was 'bout three years overdue from collapsing, but them folk in Charleston didn't care. They always said, 'We gonna get right on it.' And never done nothing.

"This bridge was so bad that one of the rules 'mongst the crew was that you couldn't eat no beans eight hours 'fore we was set to cross it."

The man looked o'er at me and said, "You know why?"

I couldn't figger what eating beans had to do with crossing no bridge, so I shrugged my shoulders.

"It's 'cause if you farted whilst the locomotive was on the bridge, you'd knock the whole thing into the river."

Me and all the other men at the fire, 'cept for the cap'n, busted out laughing.

Ol' Jerry said, "Now, once one 'em trains go down off a bridge, there ain't no one in the locomotive who ever lives, and if you ain't lucky 'nough to get snuffed out soon's you hit, the chances is good you gonna die in a horrible way, either pinned to the boiler and cooked, or having the coals spilt out on you to slow-roast you on the spot.

"Well, all the crews knowed this Hamburg bridge was one sneeze away from going down, so what we used to do was, right afore we crossed, the engineer would stop the train, lock the Johnson bar, and set the locomotive's idle on low so that the train would jus' creep along at two, three mile a hour.

"Then he'd jump off, walk 'crost the bridge, and wait for the train to roll o'er, at which time he'd jump back on board and get her rolling again.

" 'Cepting for the darkies what worked serving folk, the whole crew done the same and walked to the other side, then jumped back on once the train safely crossed.

"And wouldn't you know it, one perfect clear day, no wind, no rain, no nothing but sunshine, soon's the crew walked 'crost that bridge and turned to wait on the train to follow, someone on board must've farted; there was one big crack and down goes six cars, twenty-seven passengers, six darkies, and not one single crew member. The explosion when that boiler hit the water finished off anyone who was unlucky 'nough to survive the fall.

"Well, sirs, we was stunned. After we all give a hearty cheer and congratulates ourselves on being so smart, we seent the problem we was gonna have 'splaining to the company and the law what happened.

"Well, not so much 'splaining what happened but 'splaining why it didn't happen to no one in the crew.

"Some wanted to draw straws and pick

three crew members to get knocked in the head and throwed into the river to balance things off so's it wouldn't look so bad, but 'the devil's in the details' and whilst everyone was happy to be a head knocker or a body tosser, the list of volunteers to get head-knocked or body-tossed didn't have no names at all on it.

"So what we done was in-ducted seven of the dead passengers to be members and stand in for our corpses.

"Once one 'em locomotives jump the track and hit the water, everyone inside it gets turnt into large pieces of fried chicken, so identifying bodies wasn't gonna be something no one put too much effort in.

"We pult it off, the company was kind 'nough to notify our families and supply each one of 'em with a great big crispy piece of meat in a box for burying.

"I didn't have the nerve to do it, but I hear a couple of the other fellas wore disguises and went to their own funerals so's they could see what folk really thought of 'em. I couldn't unna-stand what good that information was gonna do 'em. I was jus' grateful for getting a second chance at making a new life for myself.

"I 'membered thinking at the time 'tis too bad this can't be a reg'lar part of living, where we all gets a chance to walk away from whatever train wreck we's made of our lives and run off to start up building something new."

He looked off to the side and spit.

"Only trouble with that is all you end up doing is building that same old life back again. You jus' a actor moving on to another performance. You might get a different group of characters, a different set, but in the end you's starring in the same old stinking play.

"One morning you gonna wake up and wonder who was the lucky ones, them that went down with the train and was snuffed out quick, or them that lived on and was having to get *their* train wreck played out slow over years and years."

For the first time since we'd been traveling, the cap'n laughed a real laugh and said, "And with that bit of mirth I'm gonna read my Bible.

"Good night, gennel-men."

O'er the next few days, I *was* able to pick me a few kernels of corn out the crap the cap'n kept dishing out.

For a sample, thieving's got one of the Ten Commandments all to itself, which means it's high up on the things that Jesus don't want you to do, higher up than tossing a sack full of whining kittens in the river or pissing down your neighbors' wells or tricking someone that's a known dimwit into giving you their shoes.

That meant the righteous, Christian thing about going north with Cap'n Buck was that by bringing thieves back to pay for their sins, we's helping to right a great wrong. That, the cap'n said, was why what we's setting out to do was more than doing good work, it was doing the Lord's work.

I's having to remind myself of that particular hard with each passing sunrise that took us closer to them thieves and farther off from Possum Moan and the last time Cap'n Buck took a bath.

I know some folk might say I'm too prissy 'bout it, 'cause don't too many summer months get away from me without one bath in 'em, but being that cleanly is a part of my nature.

I couldn't tell you where that peculiarity come from 'cause don't neither Pap nor Ma get bothered by being around folk that's smelling ripish. Or, truth tolt, they don't get upset by being odoriferous their own selfs.

But even someone whose nose ain't sensitive couldn't help but take notice of the smells the cap'n's churning out. I got some good 'spicions that the cap'n's last bath hadn't happened months afore he went off shopping at that market in Charleston. He must be one 'em folk that believe it's bad luck to take a bath in May, June, July, or August, plus any month that's got the letter *r* in its spelling.

So, far as this being the Lord's work, I was going to take his word for it, 'cause it jus' didn't sum up that nothing holy would be tied up in something that smelt this bad.

If someone was hunting *us* down 'stead of vice the versa, they wouldn't even need no genu-wine, first-rate, blue-ribbon blood-hound to pick up our trail; even a twenty-year-old, half-dead porch mutt with a snout full of snot wouldn't have no problems pointing out which direction the cap'n come from and which way he was heading, not even in a hurricane.

And it didn't matter how many hints and 'couragements I laid out to him, he jus' didn't want no truck with water and soap. Best I could figger, we'd been on this journey for two, three weeks and other than a quick dunking if we'd misestimated the depth of a river, the cap'n hadn't been nowhere close to letting nothing wet but things that come out his own body wash o'er him and his clothes.

One the times when we was pulled up for the night near a stream and I was swishing my clothes through the water and using clay for soap, I took a risk and decided to talk to him. I said, "You know, sir, since I'm already doing it, I wouldn't mind running some water o'er something of yourn too."

He looked at me slant-eyed and said, "Boy, this partnership gonna come to a quick and ugly end if I gets one more indycation you's got some interest in seeing me out my clothes."

I said, "Why, no, sir, I ain't got no interest in that, not at all. I'm jus' thinking some water might loosen up your clothes a bit. You might be more com-fitted if they wasn't so stiff and would bend easy in the places where most folks' clothes bend."

Good sense stopped me from saying it, but the man smelt worst than something warm that dropped out the south end of a sick northbound goat.

He leant up on his elbow and looked me dead in my eye and said, "There you go again, acting interested in me and my clothes. You best watch yourself, boy, I ain't use to brooking no sass from no youngsters, I don't care how big you is. And I don't mean maybe."

I ain't no fool, so I let that sleeping dog lay.

I was jus' gonna have to be content trying to always ride upwind of the ol' cap'n. Either that or find something thick and suitable for blocking up both my nose holes.

CHAPTER 8

Into Dee-troit

I ain't saying it's 'cause all the encouraging I done to get him to wash hisself, but the night after I'd tolt him 'bout bathing, I sure did get a surprise.

All the sudden I was awake. It was late and the moon was playing hide-and-go-seek with some puffy dark clouds, making the woods and the shadows slide 'twixt different shades of gray. The fire had gone cold and the horses was where they's s'pose to be, still tied to a poplar tree.

It didn't 'pear nothing was wrong, but something'd woke me just as sure as I'd got my name called.

It was the quiet.

I'd growed so accustomed to the cap'n's grunting and making noises whilst he was sleeping that when them sounds quit, it caused me alarm.

The only place he coulda gone was the river, so I cut through the woods to find him.

When I was right on the river, I heard some low sounds, so I stood behind a tree and took me a peek.

The moon got hid again and I really couldn't see nothing.

When the clouds eased up and let loose of the moon's light, I could see the cap'n plain and clear.

He'd took off his shirt and was standing waist-deep in the river, slowly splashing water up on hisself.

'Cepting for his hands and neck and face, the cap'n's skin was white as the belly of something dead, but what really drawed my eyes was his chest. There was a whole set of bumps and knobs all along his ribs.

I'd seent this afore in Possum Moan; when you summed it up with his bow legs, these was signs that someone had got a bad dose of rickets when they was young.

Standing there all aglow and lumpity-chested, he 'peared to be something that drugged itself off the bottom of the river 'stead of something that'd walked out into it.

His gun belt was looped under his arm

and 'round his neck, with the holster and pistol hanging behind him on his back.

'Twas easy to see he hadn't had much practice at this washing stuff; he didn't even bother to rub the water 'gainst his skin, he jus' let it roll offen him. Plus, if he'd-a took his hat off and used it to scoop up the water, he coulda got a whole lot more on him than the splashes his tiny hands was cupping up.

And I ain't got no idea how he thought water by itself was gonna loosen up the grease and filth that was clinging on him; he needed strong soap, and lots of it, to even start to break the grip that mess had on him.

The cap'n finally give up on pretending he was trying to wash hisself. He give a long hard sigh and his shoulders sagged whilst he put his hands o'er his eyes. His head rolled back on his neck and his mouth come open, making a quiet moan.

'Twas easy to see he was toting a harsh burden. 'Twas almost 'nough to make you feel sorry for him.

Almost.

I don't know how it happened so fast, but one second I'm looking at the cap'n and starting to feel something for him and the next I'm staring down the barrel of his pistol.

The cap'n said, "Show yourself or I'll

blow you clean into the next district."

I done what I was tolt.

I throwed my hands up and cried out, "It ain't no one but me, Cap'n! Don't shoot!"

He kept the pistol on me with his right hand and waded to the shore where his shirt was, but what he done with his left hand brung back something I'd forgot I remembered.

I wasn't but three or four at the time, a tad too young to work the land proper. I woke up one morning and, thinking they was already in the fields, I went to finish my sleeping in Ma and Pap's bed.

The curtain was still dividing the room and when I pult it aside, I was surprised to see Ma standing there without no clothes on.

We both give a yell, and Ma reached down to get her frock with her right hand and, spreading the fingers on her left hand, she put 'em 'crost her chest.

The cap'n was doing the 'zact same thing, 'cept that Ma hadn't wanted no one to see her chests, whilst the cap'n didn't want no one to see his rickets.

Keeping the gun level on me, he rasseled hisself into his shirt. I done the same thing I done when I'd seent Ma nekkid; I turnt my head away to give him his privacy.

I couldn't believe how vexed he was.

"You gonna get yourself kilt sneaking up on folk, boy."

"Sir, I wasn't doing nothing of the sort; I jus' woke up and wondered where you was at."

He was standing in my face, and started swearing at me, close 'nough that clumps of slob was jumping off the hairs covering his mouth, splashing foulness all o'er my face. But I didn't care, the pistol that was pressed 'gainst the side of my head was snatching up all my 'tention.

Without no warning at all, the cap'n quit yelling, pult the pistol out my face, and brung it o'er his head. I knowed better than to reach my hands up; I didn't want to give him no cause for thinking I was trying to grab his gun.

I stood there looking down at him, staring dead in his eyes, a-waiting on the pistol-whipping to commence.

But 'stead, the cap'n froze.

I ain't never in my life seent no one who 'peared to be so flummoxed.

He brung the pistol down to his side and started up sputtering.

"What the . . . What is that look you got on your face, boy?"

I didn't know I had no particular look on

my face; how was you s'pose to look when you was 'bout to get beat down by a gun?

"You think I ain't seent that look afore? Has you really got the gumption to stand there bold-face and look at me with pity? *Pity?*"

It wasn't till he said it that I knowed it was the truth. Since he'd first come to our door, looking for his fifty dollars, I hadn't been looking at the cap'n with nothing but scairtness, but once I seent how low and mournful and twisted up he was in the moonlight, how wore down and weary he was, I knowed he was right. I couldn't feel nothing but pity for this sad old man.

He yelled, "Is you blind, boy? You and all your kin ain't nothing but a half step better than darkies and you got the nerve to look at me with pity in your eyes? How the hell is some sharecropping, stupid, no-reading orphan boy got the nerve to pity me? Me!"

He finally pult the pistol off me and walked away.

It didn't sink in on me right then, it ain't easy to think 'bout nothing when you's had a gun drawed on you, but I sure coulda saved myself a lot of trouble if I'd been listening jus' a little carefuller to what the cap'n tolt me.

I stayed awake the rest of the night and so

did the cap'n.

When day broke and we et, wasn't a word passed 'twixt us; we just clumb back on the horses and headed out on the road north.

Jus' when I was getting use to the rise and fall of riding with the cap'n, he axed this group of folk heading south if we was on the right road for Dee-troit and how far it was.

We seent we wasn't 'bout to get no bad steering when, 'stead of having to stop and scratch their heads and try to do some figgering, the folk said, "Keep straight 'head and you'll be there in half a day."

All my imaginings 'bout settling Pap's debt and rustling up this gang that robbed the Tanners started gnawing at me and I was getting more and more excited and worked up.

But as we rode into the city, my excitement started getting wore away.

We come in from the south on a street someone tolt the cap'n was called Fort Street.

There wasn't no forts on the street but that wasn't the peculiarest thing about it.

What was odd was that you couldn't smell no grass nor trees nor even soil. 'Twas like a blanket had got dropped o'er the whole stretch, smothering the life outta everything, like someone was holding a grudge 'gainst the plants and weeds and all else that was green. It was right unbearable.

And the sounds, which started out peculiar and interesting, soon turned into being the sort of confusion that made you want to clamp your hands 'crost your ears.

Folks was yelling one after the 'nother, wagons and horses' hoofs was making sharp clacking sounds on the bricks that covered up the road, hammering and banging was coming from each direction.

As we rode down Fort Street deeper into the city, there was houses and every once in the while a building or two. The farther we rode, the less houses there was and the more buildings until the houses quit altogether, leaving one building or store or shop after the next.

They was finally crowding one into the 'nother. Where there use to be the normal proper space 'tween buildings, they soon started bumping shoulders 'gainst each other. Fighting to make sure not even a starved-out cat could squeeze 'twixt 'em. The only spaces was when a street interrupted the wall of buildings.

'Twas like the land had done something foul or turrible and every street and every building and every road was serving to make it pay by holding it put, fighting to keep what was normal and proper chained down.

The way the walls and buildings rose up brung to mind the chutes at the slaughterhouse where pigs and such was drove deeper and deeper to where the throat slitting took place.

The cap'n didn't have to worry none 'bout me wanting to stay in the city; this place had already died and was jus' a rotting corpse. I wouldn't stay here one minute past what I was being forced to.

How could anyone live here? With no trees, no birds nor other free critter, no water, just noise and buildings that made you feel you was this close to dying.

Dee-troit was huge! And colored folk was walking 'long on their merry way to who knowed where.

The cap'n axed the first white people we seent where the sheriff's office was.

He decided to start talking to me again. "When you come in someone else's backyard, you got to show 'em some respect and let 'em know what you up to. I been tolt the sheriff ain't no Yankee, so we might be in luck."

We fount the sheriff's office and pushed open the building's door and went in.

Sitting 'round a desk that was covered with newspapers and a cut-in-half tin can fulled up with cigar butts was two men. One was stout and old and the other'n was younger and skinny and stingy-looking.

The cap'n said, "Evening, gennel-men, how y'all doing?"

The old man set his newspaper down, grinned wide, and said, "I ain't doing nowhere near's good as y'all. From the song of your voice, y'all must've left South Carolliney a hour or so ago. I ain't been down home in twenty-three years, so you knows you doing better'n me."

The cap'n said, "Wasn't but three weeks ago we was there."

The old man said, "It sure do feel good to hear someone who don't talk funny! Where'bouts y'all from?"

"I'm from the Tanner plantation in the Richland District. This boy's from Possum Moan."

The man reached his hand out and shook ourn.

"Sheriff Glenn Turner's the name. This here's Keegan. Caint say I heard of neither one 'em places, but welcome to Dee-troit."

The Keegan man jus' looked at us and nodded his head. His eyes had the same dead-water look as the cap'n's.

The Dee-troit sheriff said, "Anything I can do for y'all?"

"Thank you kindly, sir. I'm knowed as Cap'n Buck and this here's Little Charlie Bobo. We's looking to get holt of some darky reprobates that run off. They been living up here for nigh on ten years. I'm letting you know as a courtesy what my intentions is here case there's some trouble."

"I do 'preciate that. Ever since them fools in Washington passed them Slave Acts, some folk come busting up here looking to grab any darky they run 'crost. Next thing I know, I'm having to file papers on dead folk, both black and white."

So it was slaves that had stole four thousand dollars from the Tanners and run off with it! I couldn't help wondering how much of the money would be left after ten years.

The sheriff said, "Who is it y'all looking for?"

"There's three of 'em, a buck and a wench in their late thirties, their boy gotta be 'round twelve now."

"What's they names?"

"The ma and pa is Lou and Cletus, the boy is Sylvester. All with the last name of Tanner."

The man shook his head. "Ain't ringing

no bells with me. Keegan?"

"Nope."

Sheriff Turner said, "But that don't mean nothing. Dee-troit's got more'n forty thousand people; yours is probably laying low. Them darkies that come from the South don't cause us no problems at all, so we don't never have no contact with 'em.

"Plus, they probably gone and changed their names. That's the first thing they want to do once they bust loose.

"Afore we get to sorting 'em darkies out, let's get your hosses took care of. Y'all staying anywhere yet?"

"We passed a boardinghouse that didn't look too bad. We'll stay there till our business is done."

"That's fine. Come on back to the stables and we can get your hosses took care of."

The sheriff pushed hisself away from the table and led us outside.

Once he seent Spangler and the cap'n's mare, he whistled. "My, my, my, them's two fine, fine hosses. Y'all must be from one the big plantations."

I could see the cap'n's hackles raising up.

"It's big 'nough."

"Cotton? Rice?"

The cap'n's good side had got wore down by the few questions the sheriff was axing.

He ignored the man. I couldn't unna-stand why; the man didn't have to help put our horses up but done it anyway. Being friendly couldn't hurt nothing.

The cap'n said, "So how much we owe y'all for tending to the horses?"

The man answered, "Let's jus' call it good old-fashioned Southern hospitality being served up a long way from home."

"Thank you, sir. Now's there somewhere near where we can get fed?"

After we got the horses stabled and bid the Dee-troit lawmen a good night, me and the cap'n walked toward where the sheriff said we could eat cheap.

I axed him, "How come you didn't tell the sheriff you got a address where the gang's hiding out? He could've tolt us where it's at."

"What," the cap'n said, "and let them two run off 'head of us and grab 'em? No, thanks.

"Maybe you ain't as dense as I first pegged you. You had sense 'nough to keep your mouth heshed back there, but I seent the foolish look on your face; don't tell me you couldn't see what was o-ccuring?"

"I thought he was jus' trying to be helpful and was jib-jabbing to pass the time."

He give me a disappointed look.

"You's every bit as dense as I first thought.

"First thing you got to keep in mind is you needs be suspicious of anyone who's looking to be helpful. Most times they ain't doing nothing but looking to help they own self.

"Second thing is chitchatting, and I s'pose even the way y'all in Possum Moan say it, 'jib-jabbing,' is how most folks is gonna feel you out afore they decide if you's worth whatever trouble they got planned to visit on you.

"And third, whenever someone starts right off getting false-friendly with you, keep in mind all they trying to do is get a leg up on you so they can know what's the best way to fleece you.

"That sheriff, who ain't nothing but a common thief with a badge, would jus' as soon stab you in the back on a lark as give you the time of day. And the other one, after five minutes of being 'round him, if you was wearing drawers, you'd have to check to make sure you still had 'em on.

"The more you keep them two highway-men in the dark, the better off you is. You jus' got the royal treatment and don't have clue the first 'bout it.

"Let's get the horses."

He opened his wallet and pult a piece of

paper out that had some scribbling on it.

"We needs find out where this address is; I gots to stop in this store to 'range for meeting the boy who gonna let us know 'zactly where our folks is at."

CHAPTER 9

The Informer

We fount the store on the paper and the cap'n tolt me to wait whilst he went in and talked to a man setting at a counter. Some money changed hands, then the cap'n headed back out to me.

"There's s'pose to be a park with a statue 'bout half a mile from here. Someone's gonna get the boy a message and he's gonna meet us there in a hour."

We set right off for the park.

The statue was of a glummish-looking man who was made of iron. I couldn't blame him for looking so low-down and beat; it 'peared every bird in Dee-troit had a job of stopping by each day and doo-dooing on him. He had a fancy old hat on his head and was carrying the kind of spear they use to chuck at folks in the Bible.

After the longest time, a colored man in a white coat covered with smears and specks of blood walked into the park and come right to us.

The colored man's boots was stained with blood and gore too. He had to work in a slaughterhouse. He'd rolt the cuffs of his trousers up, but they was stiff with dried-up blood too.

He set on the bench next to me.

"Howdy."

I knowed the cap'n was discom-fitted by the colored man setting hisself next to us without axing permission.

He never looked in the man's direction but said, "What you want, boy?"

The man shot the cap'n a dirty look.

"*Boy?* Maybe I got the wrong folk."

He got up from the bench and started walking 'way.

The cap'n smiled and called, "What's your hurry, my good man?"

The man turnt back.

"I knows you the ones from down south; who else would be sitting here looking so country?"

I guess the cap'n seent who had the upper hand here and changed his attitude.

"Why, sure we is, where you from?"

"It ain't important. You brang the money?"

The cap'n said, "Now holt on for a minute; let's see what we's paying for."

"Soon's I get the money, you'll see."

The cap'n reached in his coat pocket and set a bundle of cash on the bench.

The colored man reached o'er and began counting it out loud.

". . . thirty-five, forty, forty-five, fifty, fifty-five, sixty."

The cap'n said, "That good?"

"That's what we 'greed on."

"Well?"

The man said, "You read?"

The cap'n said, "Do you?"

The man said, "Here's what you needs."

He set a folded piece of paper on the bench where the cap'n had put the money. The cap'n pulled a face and picked it up and read what it had to say.

"I still got some questions. They lives in a two-room house at 541 Madison Street?"

"Right."

"What kinda neighborhood is it?"

"*What kind of neighborhood is it?* You looking to grab these here folk or is you looking to move in?"

"I meant is it all slaves or is it mostly white?"

"*Slaves?* Ain't no slaves here in Mitchagain."

116

"Is the neighborhood mostly white folk or colored?"

"It's a mix."

"It say she work at Seifert's Laundry, 22 Vernor, and he work at 113 Gray-tiotte; how close is they?"

"Three block apart."

"How far's that from the jail?"

"Ten-minute walk."

"Through what kinda neighborhood?"

"All businesses. All white."

"I guess that conclude our business."

The colored man said, "Maybe not. How much you willing to pay for information on two more?"

The cap'n said, "I ain't looking to be burdened by no big coffle of slaves. I'm here to get these folk only."

"The two I'm talking 'bout is your runaway's babies. Two girls. Twins. Two year old."

The cap'n said, "Healthy?"

"Fat as a couple of spring piglets."

The cap'n smiled. "Well, that do make a difference. Let's talk."

I walked up to get a better look at the statue.

They talked a bit more, the cap'n counted out some more bills, then the bloody colored man counted 'em and said, "Reach me the paper back."

He pult a pencil from behind his ear and wrote something down. "The babies stays with this woman whilst the folks is at work. That's her address. You got any more questions? I needs to get back to work."

I thought this would be when the cap'n let this man know what he thought of the disrespectful way he answered a white man's questions. But he didn't say nothing 'sides, "Thank you kindly. I'll be seeing you again soon."

"Not if I see you first."

The cap'n smiled. "I'll keep that in mind; you might be surprised."

He waved me o'er. "Follow him."

"Won't it be easier to jus' find out where the slaughterhouse is at 'round here?"

The cap'n said, "He don't work in no slaughterhouse."

"Why, sure he do, didn't you see —"

"Didn't you see the pencil?"

"Why, yes, sir, but —"

"What would someone who work in a slaughterhouse need a pencil for? To write farewell notes for the cows? To pass on any last word the sheeps had to say to their families back on the farm? To get addresses offen the pigs so's he could send postcards?

"He work in a butcher shop and I need to

know which one. If this address he give me don't pan out, me and that boy got some more talking to do. Now get moving."

"But what if I get lost?"

"Ain't no one in Dee-troit who don't know where the jail is; if you ain't back in a hour, meet me there."

I didn't have to worry. I should've knowed the cap'n would be right.

I followed the man until he went in the back of a butcher shop six blocks from the park.

There was two colored boys sitting out front of the place and I axed 'em, "What's the name of this here shop?"

They looked at one the 'nother and the skinniest one said, "Butcher shop."

"But who own it?"

"The butcher."

They laughed and I felt myself getting red.

A woman walked past and I said, " 'Scuse me, ma'am, what's this here shop called?"

She said, "The Irish Butcher Shop."

She give me a staring-down-her-nose, raising-up-her-eyebrows look and said, "You need to get back in school, young man."

I said, "Yes, ma'am," but I was thinking what I *really* needed to do was get back to South Carol-liney, where folk don't act so strange and uppity.

I walked back to the park feeling mighty low and dim.

But once me and the cap'n got back to the boardinghouse and he started planning how we was gonna catch the gang of thieves, I mostly forgot 'bout how rude these Yankees was.

It was getting more and more exciting, 'specially when the cap'n tolt me the leader of the gang was a woman that wore a eye patch and had a long scar running 'crost her forehead and cheek from when she lost the eye.

I was too worked up to sleep more'n a minute that night!

Chapter 10

Catching the Thieves!

Sweat was pouring from every part of my body.

I kept going o'er my part; I wanted to get everything jus' the way the cap'n had 'splained it. I wasn't 'bout to do none of what he called "improvising nor improving"; he'd kept drilling in me that things had to go A-B-C and if they did we'd be all right.

We'd been standing in the alley for the longest time afore he finally said, "Don't turn now, that's her with the sack and the bonnet."

The cap'n had me as a shield, ducking behind me so the woman couldn't see him. Soon's she walked on by the alley he give me a shove and I was on the sidewalk behind the woman.

Following the plan, I run out in the street till I was ten yards past, then turned to face her.

I said, " 'Scuse me, ma'am, do you know where —"

Both me and the woman gasped. I thought the cap'n had made a mistake, 'cause whilst this woman did have a eye patch and a scar running 'crost her cheek, he hadn't said nothing 'bout her skin! She was colored!

How could a woman who didn't look no different than the slaves I'd seent 'round Possum Moan be the leader of a gang that robbed Mr. Tanner of four thousand dollars?

Before I had much of a chance to think on it, something 'bout me tolt her I was trouble and she squozed the bag to her chest and done a quick look 'round.

I said, "Do you know where a stranger can get —"

She turnt back to me and at that second the cap'n eased out from the alley. I flinched when a loud crack exploded from behind the woman's back.

Time slowed down and she jerked whilst a fine red mist rose up offen her back and settled 'crost her head and shoulders.

The woman's mouth come open and she said, "Oh!"

She stumbled forward and fell in my arms.

I couldn't believe what I jus' seent! The cap'n never said nothing 'bout shooting no woman in the back!

I eased her to the ground and looked back at the cap'n; I knowed he was no good, but who could put a bullet in someone who wasn't even holding on to a knife?

I twisted the woman so's I was 'twixt her and the cap'n, hoping with all my might since he'd have to go through me, he'd hold on to his fire.

I looked into his eyes to see if he'd do it, but it didn't take but a second for me to unna-stand what happened.

The cap'n wasn't clutching on to no pistol; 'stead, in his hand was the cowhide whip that was always coiled on his saddle.

The whip was laying in front of him stretched out and resting like it was a rattler that had got a good bite in on someone.

It had made the same sound as a small pistol.

The sack the woman had been toting fell when she got hit and everything in it was spreading out willy-nilly on the sidewalk. There was apples, some collard greens, four or five tin cans, and a package that spilt; it coulda been cornmeal.

The cap'n yelled at me, "Has you lost your

mind? Move 'way from that wench, boy, or you'll be getting a taste of the lash too."

The woman was starting to get back her unna-standing of where she was.

She sat up and looked at the cap'n.

He said, "Surprise! Guess what, Lou? It been ten years and I hates saying it, but 'em years ain't been kind to you, my darling. You looking downright turrible!"

From her hands and knees, the woman started gathering the things that come out from her bag, scooping 'em in toward her.

The cap'n said, "Uh-uh, ain't no need for none of that, Lou."

The woman fount her voice. "My name ain't Lou, it's Eloise."

The cap'n laughed. "Well, a rose by any other name, huh? You jus' let Little Charlie pick them things up, you get on back here in this alley. You partial to jewelry? I knows you is, so I brung a special bracelet for you; crawl on over here and get it, girl."

The woman stood up and walked to the cap'n, a bloody slash run 'crost her back up onto her shoulder.

My hands was shaking, but I picked up her groceries, putting 'em in the sack, then went back into the alley.

The cap'n already had the woman shack-led at the ankles and the wrists. He'd made her squat down with her back to us and her face mashed into the alley's wall.

"Now we wait. The butcher said if she ain't there right at twelve thirty, the man gonna think she been tied up" — the cap'n looked at the woman and bust out laughing — "or chained up, as the case may be, at the laundry and *he* come o'er to see her. We got 'bout fifteen minutes."

Time was acting strange again and the fifteen minutes the cap'n spoke of didn't take but seconds.

The cap'n had his back to the street but kept taking looks o'er his shoulder at the place the man worked.

"Right on time!"

He stepped back into the alley and said, "Now, Little Charlie!"

I walked into the street and seent the other gang member. He was colored too and just a bit shorter than Pap but a whole lot broader.

When he 'bout got to the alley, I said, " 'Scuse me, sir, your wife tolt me to tell you she need some help o'er there."

Soon's he heard my voice, the man's eyes got wide and his nose flared.

Dropping down into a crouch, he looked at the alley and seent the cap'n and the woman standing together. The cap'n's left hand was yanking rough on the woman's hair, pulling her head backward, and his right hand was clamped on his pistol, which was jammed under her chin and pointed upward.

"Easy, now, big boy. Let's think 'bout this."

The man said, "He hurt you, 'Loise?"

"Naw, honey, I'm doing fine. He can't do nothing to me."

The big black man seent the pickle they was in and knowed there wasn't nothing he could do. His shoulders sagged and a low, soft moan come outta him.

"Atta boy. Now jus' get down on your knees and come into the alley."

The man done it.

"Lay on your belly."

The man leant forward till he was flat on the ground.

The cap'n turnt the woman loose and slammed his boot onto the man's head, pinning him to the ground.

"Little Charlie, gimme them shackles."

I picked the heaviest set of shackles outta the bag and handed 'em to the cap'n.

"All right, Cletus. You know your right from your left? Put your right hand behind your back nice and slow."

The man did.

The cap'n grabbed holt of the man's fore-arm.

He put the top half of the shackle on the man's wrist and locked it down. Hard.

He pushed it even harder, till it was biting into the man's black skin, making all the veins in his hand bulge like thick, black night crawlers.

"Now, boy, the other hand."

He done it again.

"Raise your left foot."

The cap'n got the shackle on his ankle.

"The other'n."

The man was completely shackled on his belly.

The cap'n tolt me, "Push her back in the alley."

I led the woman to the back of the alley. The cap'n unwound his bullwhip and it runged out three times, opening three perfect straight lines 'crost the man's back.

The man flinched but never cried out.

The cap'n put his pistol on the man and walked o'er to where I was holting the woman.

He put his hand in the pockets on her apron and come out with some coins and a ratty old folded-up piece of paper. He opened it and laughed.

"Well, looky here, Little Charlie Bobo; we

gots to set this woman a-loose. These here official papers says she been granted her freedom by her master, one Mr. Robert Boylar, eight year ago."

The cap'n ripped the paper into bits.

"Who you think this was gonna fool, Lou?"

He reached his hand down the front of her smock and snatched a chain and locket offen her neck. He unclasped the locket and laughed.

"Well, well, well! Three locks of curly darky hair. Ain't that adorable?"

He slid the locket and chain into his pocket.

He bent o'er the man and went through his pockets too. There wasn't nothing.

The cap'n give the man a kick to the ribs and said, "Now get up."

The man struggled to get to his feet. When he done it, he towered o'er the cap'n.

Pointing with his pistol, the cap'n gestured for the man to start walking.

We turnt into a parade as we left the alley. The man was up front, the cap'n behind him, then the woman with me behind her.

The cap'n tolt the man, "Move smart to the left."

There wasn't many folks on the street, but every one we seent, both black and white, first give us looks of surprise that turnt dirty a second or two after. But no one didn't say nothing nor raise a finger to stop us.

We started walking toward the jail; I was praying we wouldn't draw no 'tention, but that was nigh on impossible when you's got two bloody darkies and one scairt-looking white boy 'long with a nervous, dirty, stringy white man pushing 'em forward.

Plus, the woman who was the leader of the thieves wasn't having none of being quiet. She had things she wanted to say and wasn't 'bout to be stopped.

She called out to the chained colored man, "We knowed, my sweet, my precious. We knowed.

"There ain't been one second in these pass nine and a half year that we wasn't a-waiting this. We done had us 'most ten year to get ready, so this ain't no surprise. We knowed it was coming. We knowed it would end.

"But, Chester, my beloved, each day it didn't happen was Christmas, it didn't matter what the month."

The cap'n said, "You shet your mouth, Lou."

She wasn't having none of it.

"I knowed it wasn't but a matter of time afore I'd turnt a corner, or opened a door, or would jus' be going 'bout my business walking down the street and the cap'n was gonna be there, waiting, the cap'n or some other piece of stank garbage."

The cap'n hissed, "Lou, if you don't shet up, it's gonna be hard on you, I swear it!"

She laughed. "What you gonna do? You gonna damage Massa Tanner's goods? Shoot me, I don't care."

She kept talking. "But, Chester, them was nine and a half good years, real good years, years we didn't have no right to nor 'spectations from.

"I tells you this every day, but it still ain't 'nough, honey; you's been the best man someone could love, you's the strongest, kindest, gentlest person there is and you knows how much I love you, my sweet."

"Lou! You hesh up right now."

"My name's Eloise. Eloise Demarest. And that fine man there is my husband. Mr. Demarest, don't you hang your head, my love, not for one minute. We done the best things folks can do up here and we had us all them years of heaven.

"And we stolt every last second of 'em from them Tanners! And ain't no way they can get 'em back neither."

The cap'n reached back and cuffed her in the face.

She spit blood and said, "Jus' 'member, my dear, my beloved, that this ain't us no more. We's done, we's through, but we's done the best folk can do and we's gonna live on, we's sent three tidings to live on."

I don't think no one in the world was ever happier to see a jail than I was when we turnt a corner and the Dee-troit jail was jus' a block away.

But the excitement wasn't done; a colored woman called from 'crost the street, "Don't you fret, Eloise, I knows what to do. They's gonna be all right."

The woman bust out in tears and run back the way we'd come from.

I looked at the cap'n.

He said, "Don't worry none 'bout her; long afore she get back, these two will be cooling their heels in a cell."

When we got back to our boardinghouse, I felt as dirty as if I'd been riding behind the cap'n for a month. No 'mount of soap was making me feel better. I had to bite down hard on a washrag so's the cap'n wouldn't hear me crying.

❧ Chapter 11 ❧

Savages

The cap'n was in a bad temper; I'd slept later than I ever had in my life and he woke me by slamming his boots into the wall. He'd already been out to check on the address where them twins was s'pose to be and the place was a cobbler shop owned by a white man who didn't know nothing 'bout no colored twin babies. The man from the butcher shop had tricked the cap'n outta fifty dollars, quit his job, and hightailed it to who-know-where.

Next we went to check on the house where the slaves we'd caught on the street was s'posed to be living.

No one answered the cap'n's knocks.

The door was real thin and the cap'n shouldered it open with one bump.

Soon's we were in, he put the sawed-off

132

shotgun next to the door and looked 'round.

The inside of the house was a real surprise, nothing like a place some slaves was living in for ten years. It was one real big room sectioned off into different parts. And it was clean.

There was a eating and food-fixing part with a old-time stove and pile of wood, a sleeping part behind a curtain, a part with a table and ink bottle on it, a part with a bunch of red bricks stacked up with boards 'twixt 'em for holting up 'bout fifteen or twenty books.

Everything was wiped of dust and shining.

They didn't have much furniture, and the pieces they had wasn't nowhere near as good as me and Pap could've made, but they was solid.

There was a table for eating, four chairs — none of 'em any kin to the next one — a desk, and two peculiar chairs that 'peared to be too big to be toys but too small for real people.

There was a big sideboard with some dishes and jars and jugs of food piled neat 'crost the shelves it had. Next to the fireplace was another table, this one littler, with drawers running down one side and one long drawer running 'crost the top.

The cap'n said, "Let's make this quick. If we's lucky we'll get some clue where the boy is at."

It was almost a shame the way the cap'n set 'bout searching the thieves' home. He was more interested in busting things up than looking for clues.

He picked up every dish and jug and bottle they had, looked into 'em, shook 'em, then tossed 'em into the middle of the floor so's they shattered.

He checked every tin and jar of food, then emptied 'em on the pile of broke-up dishes; he used his boots to stomp every chair into kindling. Every broom and mop was snapped in half. The only thing he couldn't bust up was the table.

He went at the few books they had particular harsh, tearing pages out of 'em and wadding 'em into balls afore he pitched 'em on the pile.

He snorted when he picked up the last book, the Bible. He put it back.

He even pulled all the ticking out the mattress from their bed and added it to the pile of confusion he was building in the center of the room.

As much ruckus as the cap'n was making, the pounding that exploded out of the small house's only door was even louder. I near jumped out my skin when someone yelled, "Chester, Eloise, is y'all all right?"

The cap'n walked fast-fast to the door and picked up his shotgun. He reached in his coat pocket and tossed me his pistol 'stead of Pap's.

He whispered, "Stand o'er there, turn your body to the side and if it's one, aim at his head, if it's more than one, aim at the head of whoever's second in line. But don't shoot nor do nothing less'n I tells you to."

He closed his eyes and shook his head. "I pray to sweet baby Jesus that bad marksmanship ain't something that run in the Bobo family. If you's as cockeyed a shot as your ma was, my goose is cooked. And yourn too."

Even though my heart was beating my ribs to death, I still felt myself starting to blush.

"Now you watch careful what I do here; first thing is you got to grab control of the sit-a-way-shun right off, you got to be loud and let 'em know you the craziest one in the equation with the least to lose. Watch careful how I casts a spell on 'em and don't let 'em ease out of it."

The banging commenced again. "Eloise? Chester?"

The cap'n snatched the door open, causing it to come partial off the top hinge. He yelled, "Who has the nerve to interfere with me doing my legal duty?"

There was three colored men standing on the front porch, and somewhere in Dee-troit a table was leaning propped up on one leg 'cause each of the men was gripping on to one of the three missing legs to use as clubs.

The cap'n said, "What the . . ." and leveled the shotgun at the men.

You'd've thought they was trying to stop a runaway carriage; every one of 'em tossed the table's legs down and throwed their hands up in front of theyselfs whilst at the same time yelling, "Whoa! Whoa! Whoa!"

The cap'n screamed right back at 'em, "How you darkies gonna stop a white man doing his legal duty?"

The *whoa*s kept coming.

The cap'n pressed his 'vantage and flipped his lapel so's his slave-catcher badge was showing.

"Does any of y'all know how to read?"

The one up front was starting to fall outta the spell the cap'n had cast.

He said in a snotty tone whilst looking the cap'n in the eye, "We all do, do you?"

The cap'n ignored his words and said, "Then y'all can see me and my pard-nah is here on official guv-mint business."

He bobbed his head at me.

"And we can kill anyone that try to stop us from the ex-a-cution of our swore God-give duties. This here badge give us that right."

The three men looked in my direction and, seeing me for the first time, threw up another chorus of *whoa*s and took another step back.

The cap'n said, "If y'all's got any problems with what I'm doing, we can go get my cousin, Sheriff Turner, and have him set it straight. Or better yet, I can blow y'all to bits myself."

One of the men said, "Don't do nothing stupid. Come on, fellas, let's go find Gina."

They eased theyselfs off the porch, walking backward.

The cap'n shut the door the best he could and said, "We's on the clock now; folks' courage starts growing fast once they ain't at the end of the barrel of a gun; who knows what them fools is gonna talk theyselfs into doing. Hang on to that pistol."

I said, "There ain't no place in here big 'nough to be hiding four thousand dollars; maybe it's all been spent?"

The cap'n looked at me like I was a moron.

"Spent? What four thousand dollars you talking 'bout?"

"Ain't that why we chasing 'em, 'cause they stole money from Mr. Tanner?"

The cap'n shook his head. "Naw, fool, they didn't steal no money, they was worth four thousand dollars when they run 'way ten year ago. They stole they own selfs."

How could someone steal —

"Quit interfering with my work, boy. Jus' watch that door."

He went back to tearing down the house.

He attacked the table with drawers that was setting next to the fireplace, which, in my mind, if he was really looking for clues, was the first place he should've looked.

As soon as he pulled open the drawer that run along the bottom of the table, a smile starts creeping 'crost the cap'n's face.

He took out a stack of envelopes that was tied together neat with a blue ribbon.

He opened one of the envelopes, took out the letter inside, and started reading. The smile on his face growed more and more with everything he read.

The cap'n kissed the letter and said, "You know what this is, boy?"

"Yes, sir, it's a envelope."

The smile left his face. "Of course it's a envelope, you mo-ron. But it's something else too.

"It's proof that you need to learn how to

read. If it was you by yourself that come up here, this would be the end of the line for you; you'd have to go back to Mr. Tanner with jus' them two darkies that's sitting in the pokey.

"But if you hadn't-a misspent your youth chasing rabbits and possums barefoot through the hollers and learnt to read, you'd know that these here letters is the key to another fifteen hunnert dollars.

"Our third fugitive, who's going by the alias Sylvanus, has got hisself in a school 'crost the river in a place called . . ." — he looked back at the envelope — "called Saint Catharines."

He kept reading, then laughed. "Listen to this. *'I continue to do well in my studies and am first in my class in calculus and Greek. I am currently second in literature and Latin but strive daily to improve.'*

"Don't that beat all? You can't tell me that that don't make you, a free white boy in these here U-nited States of A-mur-ica, 'shamed near to death that you can't even read your own name, and this darky, who must be 'round your age, is doing Greek? That don't gall you?"

Maybe this boy could do Greek, whatever that was, but could he do something useful? Pap once tolt me he didn't think there was another twelve-year-old boy in the world who could handle a two-mule team for twelve hours straight plowing up a field.

Could the colored boy do that?

And I do know how to read my name when I see it.

The cap'n turnt the letter o'er and read from the back.

"Listen here. *'My greatest dream and wish is that someday soon I'll be able to once again return home to be held in the arms of the kindest, most loving parents a boy could ask for. Give my warmest embraces to my sisters and tell them they are constantly in their brother's prayers. Faithfully yours, your most obedient son, Sylvanus.'* "

The cap'n said, "Ooh, that there's some good writing. I wonder who helped him?"

He put the letter back in the envelope, slid it into the blue-ribbon pile with the others, then tossed it to me.

"Hang on to those; I'll read the rest when we gets back to the hotel. Maybe our Mr. Shake-a-Spear'll tell where them twin girls is."

The envelopes was all of the same kind of rough paper, but the writing on 'em was very fancy and done neat.

There was the same stamp on each one.

The cap'n's voice made me jump. "What

140

I tell you, boy? We's doing the Lord's work and at the same time granting wishes to this darky, 'cause it ain't gonna be long 'fore we's gonna put him right back in his mammy's loving arms.

"Let's get outta here afore we draw any more unwelcome guests."

As we was fixing to leave, the cap'n went back and took the Bible off the shelf.

He opened it and there was a bunch of writing all o'er the pages at the front. He read some of it and tore the pages out, then ripped 'em into pieces that fluttered to the floor. He give the writing at the back of the book the same treatment.

He set the Bible back on the table.

"Savages."

He spit on the broke-up pile of the family's goods.

"Go check the street and see if them colored boys is laying in wait."

I raised the gun and walked out of the busted door.

I helt my breath and stepped onto the sidewalk.

There wasn't no one near.

I called out, "Ain't no one here."

The cap'n come out with the shotgun in one hand and Pap's pistol in the other.

"We gotta go back to the jail; I got a few

things I needs to talk to Lou about."

When we got there, the cap'n went right to the pen where the woman was being helt.

She looked something turrible; she hadn't had no sleep at all.

The cap'n set a chair next to the bars.

"So, Lou, where's that boy y'all runned off with?"

"He died from smallpox four year back."

The cap'n smiled.

"Really?"

She didn't say nothing.

"Folks is saying you birthed a set of twins 'round a year or two pass. Where they at?"

"They died from the scarlet fever three month past."

"Ooh, let me sit a little farther 'way from you, y'all sure do seem to be toting every dis-ease knowed to man."

"It's 'cause of all that good food Massa Tanner use to feed us."

"Still ain't got rid of that smart mouth, has you, Lou? Now tell me where them girls is at."

"You must know something I don't; why don't you go find 'em?"

"That's jus' what we gonna do, soon's I get back from paying a visit to a school up in Saint Catharines, Canada.

"You see, I got me a 'pointment to meet

me a young man go by the name Mr. Sylvanus Demarest."

It was easy to see that that shook the slave
woman up; her face never changed, but her
voice was shaking when she said, "You do
what you gotta."

"You ain't really in no position to be telling no one to do nothing, is you?"

"By the smell from here, I wishes I wasn't
in no position to be near you."

My stomach started tightening up. I could
see the cap'n was itching to hit this woman
again and I didn't think I could watch that
for a third time.

He looked into her face hard, then starts
a-smiling slow.

"Don't worry, woman, I'm gonna do
'zactly what I got to. I ain't gonna be long
in Canada, and once I gets holt of that big,
smart, edy-cated boy a yourn, me and him
and you's gonna do some par-laying and
soon after our talking's done, they's gonna
have to write a new chapter for the Bible.

"I'm hoping Lazarus don't mind sharing
the spotlight, 'cause sure as shooting, after
I'm done talking to y'all, I know them dead
twins a yourn is gonna get resurrected, they
gonna shake off that scarlet fever, pop out
they graves good as new, and, hallelujah, it's
gonna be a miracle when the whole family

join up for the trip home!"

For the first time since we'd caught her on the street, the woman started 'pearing to be worried and saggish.

"If it wasn't for the fact that you done so good and made two breeding wenches for Mr. Tanner, I'd take you out back of this jail and cut your throat right here right now. But the boss man gonna be good and happy for them gifts. Who knows; you looks rough, but maybe you ain't too old to make him some more breeders."

She kept her tongue tight in her mouth.

The cap'n put his hand behind his ear and said, "What? Speak up, Lou, I caint hear you.

"That's what I thought. The time for your sassiness is past, Lou; y'all's all Mr. Tanner's property and justice done woke up."

CHAPTER 12

Fixing to Go to Canada

The cap'n tolt the Dee-troit sheriff, "We's got reason to believe the young boy done took off to Canada. What can y'all tell me's involved in running him down up there?"

The sheriff give a long whistle and said, "Sir, I wish y'all every possible bit of luck in getting him back; you sure gonna need it."

"What you mean?"

"You gonna be fishing in a complete different pond once you go 'crost that river. Why, some of them white people 'crost there's downright hostile to letting even one darky come back.

"And the runaways theyselves? Well, jus' you wait and see. I've had folk from down home tell me there ain't no words to describe what happen to them darkies once

145

they get the notion that they's free.

"I'd advise 'gainst going there, fellas; y'all'll be a couple of fish out of water. You heard that ol' joke, what do you call a Yankee in the middle of a South Carol-liney swamp?"

"What?"

"Gator food."

The cap'n didn't laugh.

The sheriff said, "You'll be jus' as outta place and jus' as lost in Canada."

The cap'n said, "I 'preciates what you saying, but my rep-a-tation's at stake here, and I ain't leaving till I seent for myself it's impossible to get this boy."

The sheriff said, "Well, gennel-men, one thing you gonna have to do if y'all insist on going through with this is . . . and I ain't meaning to be indelicate, but y'all gonna have to do some . . . uh . . . sprucing up of yourselfs."

I couldn't believe the cap'n had the gumption to set there looking like he didn't have no idea what the man was trying to say.

"What you mean?"

The sheriff said, "Well, sir, I knows y'all been on the trail for a long time and ain't had the 'vantage of bathing. All I'm saying is, if you was to go over into Canada looking as you do at the moment, you might as well tie two signs 'round yourselfs. The one up front should say, 'Slave-Catching A-mur-icans,' and the one on your back don't need no words at all; jus' paint a bull's-eye there.

"Even if you was to take off that slave-catcher badge, them Canadians would have you pegged ten seconds after y'all got off the ferry."

The cap'n was starting to catch on to what the man was saying, and wasn't finding it too pleasant. He jus' stared.

"And I'm 'suming y'all came up here flush with cash, true?"

The cap'n said, "The only reason I'm listening to you is you's from back home and been kind 'nough to holt on to them runaways for me. But this is getting a little more into my business than I'm comf-table with."

The sheriff said, "Not at all, sir. All I'm looking to do is not have y'all run on into Canada and get your heads handed to y'all on a platter. If I'm treading where I shouldn't be, I'm gonna beg your leave and hesh up right now."

The cap'n thought on it for a second, give the sheriff a weak smile, and said, "I do 'pologize, sir. It's jus' that I ain't as yet use to being up here; y'all do so many things different that I'm probably being too touchy.

I do 'preciate your 'sistance."

"My pleasure, sir, glad to help a gennel-man from the south at any time."

The cap'n said, "To answer your question, we's got all our expenses covered, plus any surprises that might present theyselfs. I'm putting myself in your hands; what would you suggest I do, sir?"

"When you planning on going?"

"Soon's possible."

"I'd strongly suggest y'all cool y'all heels for three or four days afore you go."

"Why's that?"

"Y'all's got three stops you need make, and to do everything proper's gonna take some time."

The cap'n didn't say nothing.

"First, soon's you leave here, go on down to Roma Barbershop over on Erie Street. Ax for the owner, man by the name of Clau-dio Visseli; tell him I sent y'all and you's looking for gennel-men's cuts.

"Gennel-men's. Cuts.

"You's gonna have to say good-bye to the beard and them muttonchops and that's one sure 'nough impressive moustache you got there, but it's got to be tamed down some too.

"Let Claudio do what he want. We's try-ing to get the South Carol-liney offen y'all and, much as it's gonna turn y'all's stomachs, turn y'all into a couple of Yankee Doodle dandies."

The cap'n said, "That ain't gonna take no three days to do."

The sheriff said, "That's jus' for starters, sir. Once Claudio's done with you, go right 'crost the street and get you a room with a bath at the National Hotel on Woodward.

"With. A. Bath.

"Y'all needs some tendering up. Don't camp out whilst you's waiting; y'all needs to get the road outta your bones for long as you can. Y'all won't look quite so rough and . . . well . . . so country after a couple days' rest.

"Then, once you's scrubbed yourself down good, head on over to a shop called Roderick Rowser's — he a tailor — and tell him you looking into buying you a suit. And y'all can't be cheap neither.

"Tell him I sent you and then he'll have 'em altered overnight.

"It really don't matter how much we polishes y'all up, you ain't gonna fool nobody for long, soon's you opens your mouths South Carol-liney's gonna come dripping out and once them Canadians hear that song in your voice, your goose is cooked, won't none of 'em help you with nothing. So all we gotta do is to get y'all past a quick glimpse, and that might be 'nough.

"Was you planning on taking a third hoss over to carry your package back?"

"Yes, sir, I'd planned on that."

"I'd plan on something else. The only way y'all's gonna get close to this boy without setting off all kinds of red flags is if you's to come 'crost as something y'all ain't . . ."

Showing the first signs of being alive since we come in, the Keegan man give a crooked smile and axed, "Civilized?"

The cap'n didn't smile back.

The sheriff axed, "This boy y'all's running down ain't in a place called Buxton, is he?"

"I ain't for sure; he's going to school somewhere called Saint Catharines."

"Good, good. If he was in Buxton, y'all'd have to write him off, but Saint Catharines ain't far from Niagry Falls; there's trains in and out of there all the time, and the darkies there ain't quite as unpleasant as they is in Buxton.

"So iffen it was me, I'd board my hosses at the livery here in Dee-troit, take a ferry 'crost, then get on the train and go scout out what you need to do to get holt of your boy.

"You can't be carrying no bullwhip nor no bags that anyone can tell is heavy with chains and shackles. The whole point is that things has got mighty tough on catchers that go over, so we want y'all to look different."

The cap'n didn't look happy. "So this is gonna be harder than I thought."

"I got to tell you, of every ten slave catchers that goes over, five come back with the white beat right off of 'em, four ain't never heard from again, and ain't but one come back with a darky.

"And I don't think them four that disappears got into Canada and fount the climate to be so welcoming that they retired and is spending the rest of their days growing sunflowers.

"If anything, they's supplying the sunflowers with fertilizing.

"Y'all ain't got no papers showing y'all own him, do you? That might be some help."

The cap'n grunted. "Didn't believe I'd need any. So what you think, is it best to grab him at night and wait till early morning to travel?"

The sheriff said, "That's one of y'all's options, but that's problemish too; the roads is full of people looking to disrupt what you got planned."

The cap'n shook his head.

Sheriff Turner said, "The best thing to do, and the only way I'd do it if it was me looking for someone, is to trick the boy into coming to Windsor on his own somehow. Once you get him to Windsor, it ain't nothing to bring him 'crost the river."

The cap'n said, "Look, I know you's a busy man, but I'd be willing to pay good for a couple of days of your time if you was to come over with us."

The sheriff laughed and said, "I guess that depend on how you define 'pay good.' "

I couldn't believe my ears when the cap'n said, "Five hunnert dollars if we gets him. I think your knowledge is worth every penny of that."

I couldn't believe my ears even more when the sheriff laughed and said, "Not for twice that, sir. I'm going back home in a year and a half and I don't need no more excitement than I already had. I could sure use the money, but it ain't worth the risk. That's truly a generous offer, but I gotta turn it down."

The cap'n said, "Well, I 'preciate the advice. I ain't lost no one yet; these three's the only blemish I got and I'm intending to rid myself of that."

❧ CHAPTER 13 ❧

The Big Cleanup

The barbershop was full of laughing and talking when we stepped in.

Didn't take but a second for all that to come to a end once folks seent the cap'n.

We fount ourselves two seats and waited.

There was all sorts of sharp and dangerous-looking blades and razors and knifes setting behind where the barber stood whilst he was cutting hair. But the cap'n didn't care; now that I know him a bit, I bet he was thinking the stopping of the talk was disrespecting him.

He bust out being rude as he wanted to be.

I was thinking different. I seent all them sharp tools, the skinny, steel-edge razors, the blades that could probably slice a eyebrow hair in half lengthwise, and all

153

these strange sorts of sharp, pointy scissors as reasons to be concerned 'bout the feelings of whoever it was that worked with 'em every day.

If you was sensible, you wouldn't want no one who was vexed at you swinging 'em slitting tools nowhere near your throat or lips. One slip and you'd be looking at you ear laying there 'mongst the hair and cigar butts and spitted-out tobacco juice on the barbershop floor.

And if the barber *had* cut my ear off, I'd jus' leave it laying there too. I'd grab me one 'em white towels, press it 'gainst the side of my head, and go 'bout my business without saying nothing more that would risk getting more bits of me yimmed off my body.

But the cap'n seent it different and right after the barber give us a "Good morning and welcome, gennel-men," the cap'n set in complaining and insulting loud 'nough for everyone, including the barber, to hear him.

"Fifteen cents for a haircut? Ten cents for a shave? I'll tell you what, Little Charlie Bobo, when it come time for me to pay him, hand the barber your pistol so's he can put it on me and we can say this was a honest robbery."

And he wasn't happy jus' insulting the

barber neither; he had something to say 'bout near everyone who went 'head of us.

"Much of a pinhead as you is, if I was you, I wouldn't pay no more'n half price," he said to one man.

"You ain't got but nine hairs atop your head," he said to another. "Gimme one 'em scissors and five seconds and I'll charge you jus' a nickel."

The cap'n worked o'er the barber and all the folks ahead of us for haircuts pretty good.

When it come time for one of us to go, he said, "Go 'head on, Little Charlie Bobo, I wants to see how you turns out."

I was hoping the cap'n would go outside for a second so's I could tell this barber that I didn't have nothing to do with all the nonsense he was saying, but the luck of the Bobos helt strong and he stayed put.

I clumb up in the barbering chair and he leant my neck back till it was resting on this peculiar-shape piece of wood. I was staring di-rect up at the tin ceiling of the place.

"What can I do for you?"

The cap'n tolt him, "The sheriff sent us over, and said we needed us some gennel-men's cuts."

"All right, let's see what I'm dealing with."

He pulled my hat off and said, "Oh! You're

jus' a kid."

"I'm twelve year old, sir."

"Huh, you sure are big."

"Yes, sir."

He started in cutting my hair.

When he was done, the barber handed me a looking glass and turnt the chair so's I could see the back of my own head.

I ain't being no bragger when I say I ain't never seent no handsomer lad in my whole life!

I couldn't pull my eyes offen myself.

Everything 'bout my head looked clean and crisp and shiny.

I was so proud of how good the barber made me look that I give him a big hand-shake. Without giving it no thought I just 'bout hugged the man too. But from the look on the cap'n's face I knowed 'twas best not to.

Instead I said, "Thank you very much, sir!"

He popped the sheet offen me and used his brush to wipe off my hairs that had fallen on the barbering chair.

He looked at the cap'n and said, "Sir?"

The cap'n hung his coat on a pole with hooks on it.

He made sure everyone seent him pull his

pistol and jam it into his belt afore he sat down.

The barber said, "Gentleman's cut?"

The cap'n was all the sudden quiet, he jus' nodded his head.

The barber said, "Let me see what I'm working with," and pult on the cap'n's hat, but the hat was so stuck in place it didn't want to leave the cap'n's head without some considerable pulling.

When that hat come off and I seent what it was hiding, I knowed I'd been riding with the man day and night for near three weeks and hadn't never seent him not wearing that hat! Not even whilst he was taking that bogus bath in the river.

The top of the cap'n's head was total bald! The scraggly, stringy, nasty tangle of hair that run 'round his head jus' above his ears made it look like his head was wearing a furry little coat!

But that wasn't the worst thing; starting halfway back on his forehead, the cap'n's skin went from being brown as any slave you'd see to all the sudden being so white you was tempted to shield your eyes. The whole top of his head looked like a huge chicken had laid a egg there and flewed off.

And the odd thing was the brown part of his skin was as wrinkled and creased and folded-up as a hunnert-year-old saddle, while the white part was smooth as a baby's behind.

It was the most bee-zarre sight I'd ever seent.

As hard as the cap'n had used his mouth on the innocent folks in the barbershop, this was their chance to repay him, 'cause you wouldn't-a needed no imagination at all to come up with a slew of insults to make about what he'd been keeping hid under his hat.

But that egg what was sittin' atop his head didn't do nothing but serve to make the cap'n look scarier and more de-ranged than he done afore.

The other people in the barbershop's eyes mighta been poppin' out they sockets, but no one had nothing to say.

The barber said, "Sir, I can't do anything with this until your hair's been washed."

"Well, wash it, then."

"That's going to be an extra dime."

"How'd I know that was gonna cost more? Go 'head and do it."

The barber leant the cap'n's head all the way back and set a big bowl behind the cap'n. He filt the bowl with water and put the back of the cap'n's head o'er it. He run some water out of a jug and started soaping up the cap'n's hair. The soap went from bubbly white to oily black in two seconds. The barber rinsed it out, then did it again three times afore the rinse water run clear.

Once he'd dried the cap'n's hair, he set to cutting it. When he was done, it looked like his head had took off the coat and put on a light jacket. But at least it looked neat.

Then the barber used some of them pointy killing-looking scissors to cut the cap'n's chin and muttonchops down afore he soaped 'em up and shaved 'em off. He started going at the Spanish moss moustache and the cap'n grabbed his arm.

"What you doing?"

"You said you wanted a gentleman's cut. That means no facial hair."

The cap'n thought on it for a second, then turnt the man's hand a-loose.

"You can trim it down but don't cut the whole thing off."

When the barber finished all the cutting and trimming and yimming at the cap'n, he handed him the looking glass. The cap'n wouldn't even take it. He just said, "Gimme my hat."

He put his hat back on and starts looking hisself o'er in the mirrors. Once we seent his back was turnt to us, me and everyone else in the place pult a face. I mean what kind of sense do it make to get your head cleant off for the first time in only-baby-Jesus-know how many years, then put the same dirty, stanking, nasty hat back on it?

The first thing that come to my mind was that the barber and his haircutting had busted up a bunch of lice families, them that stuck with the cap'n's hat and them that hung on to his hair and got drownded and washed away.

It was hard to believe, but the cap'n smiled, and I know for sure it was a smile 'cause most the Spanish moss moustache was now on the barbershop floor.

Chapter 14

Canada

I'd be lying if I said I wasn't worried a whole bunch 'bout going o'er into Canada. One the things you got to love 'bout A-mur-ica is that we's got laws that protects all sorts of folks from getting hurt by other folks. Canada, from what I heard so far, ain't nowhere near that civilized.

From all the things I'd been hearing 'bout it, Canada's gonna have me scratching my head more and harder than them chiggers did two year past.

I hadn't never really took no notice of the cap'n's mouth afore, but now that I was see-ing it clear, I could unna-stand why he didn't want the barber to cut his moustache down.

The cap'n had growed it long 'nough that it drooped down to cover what he had left of his teeth. They wasn't nothing but rotten green-and-black stumps poking out of his pink-and-brown-and-gray gums.

Whilst he was talking, strings of dark brownish slobber gathered up in the corners of his mouth and was getting stretched from his lower lip to his upper one with every word.

The more he talked, the thicker they got until the corners of his mouth looked as though they was being helt together by thick, sticky, brown spiderwebs.

I started thinking the barber should've listened to the cap'n; it was a real mistake to've cut that Spanish moss moustache off. I never knowed what a big favor it'd been doing everyone.

I hadn't got much sleep, but it wasn't jus' worrying 'bout Ma and Stanky and Pap that had me tossing and kicking; it was thinking 'bout what was gonna happen today.

Once the sun come up, I was gonna do a whole lot of things for the first time ever, things I ain't never dreamed of doing whilst plowing land or chasing rabbits and 'coons barefoot through the hollers outside Possum Moan.

This would be the first time I would ever ride on a boat, the first time I would ever leave A-mur-ica, the first time I would ever go to a foreign country, and best of all, the first time ever I would get to travel on a steam locomotive, something I thought only rich folk done.

I'd seent trains afore in South Carol-liney, and the way they blasted by made you wonder if they was real or just a dream; I mean the train wasn't here for one second, then it was, then it wasn't again.

The cap'n and me walked the five blocks from the livery stable to the ferry that would take us into Canada. Since we wasn't looking to be gone no more than two days, we was traveling light. I was give the chore of toting the cap'n's bag that was holting his and Pap's pistols, extra shells, the cap'n's wallet, and a light set of handcuffs, jus' in case.

We both had put on our new Sunday best jackets, trousers, shirts, and neckties, and we looked right respectful as we stepped up on the ferry.

Folks even nodded the brims of their hats at the cap'n, which surprised him much as it surprised me!

Once we got to the boat, the cap'n handed the man two dimes!

It was powerful expensive to ride on the ferry, but if didn't nothing else happen on this whole trip, I had one thing I'd be remembering and smiling o'er for the rest of my life. And I only had took me half a step outta Dee-troit.

Soon as my foot hit the floor of the ferry, a man in a fancy u-nee-form, wearing white gloves, stuck his hand out to me and said, "Watch your step, sir!"

Sir!

That was the first time in my life anyone had called me sir and I ain't but twelve year old! I wasn't sure if he said it 'cause he thought I was older than I am or if he said it to everybody. But some chirren got on after us and he didn't say nothing to 'em!

That ended up being the best thing 'bout the whole ferry ride.

The worst thing was the ride was so dog-gone short.

A bell runged and a whistle tooted and if you'd-a sneezed, you'd-a missed the whole thing. I ain't 'zactly sure what I was 'specting, but I was sure 'specting more'n jus' the whistle to toot again and the bell to get runged one more time and afore you knowed it, we'd gone and bumped into the shore of Canada.

We got off and I figgered out why the man called me sir; it was 'cause they'd feel guilty if they didn't give you something for the dime they was charging to take us 'crost.

Far's I could see, there wasn't much difference 'tween folk in Dee-troit and folk in the city called Windsor. My eye still wasn't use to seeing colored people dressed up in full sets of clothes 'stead of wearing the rags most slaves in South Carol-liney chooses to wear, but I was getting to the point where I didn't stare at 'em quite so hard; mostly I was stealing backward and sideways glances.

The Canadians had things set up real easy for you if you was traveling; the train station wasn't but a hop, skip, and a jump 'way from where the ferry let you off.

After jus' two seconds of looking at the locomotive, I knowed there wasn't gonna be nothing disappointing 'bout my first train ride!

The inside of the train was swanky as what my imaginings had tolt me the inside of the Tanners' plantation house was like. Or maybe even George Washington's! There was fancy, soft-looking seats on both sides of a little lane that run from the front of the car to the back.

A man in high-tone clothes and a round red cap shouted, "All aboard," then pult up the steps right into the train.

I sat in one of the benchy chairs and was relieved when 'stead of sitting next to me, the cap'n got in the chair right behind mine.

He was smelling lots better since he'd washed hisself off, but his odor wasn't the only thing that made him foul to sit 'round.

Besides, I'd got so use to not breathing out my nose when he was 'round that jus' looking at him got me mouth breathing and that ain't com-fitting after while.

There was seven or eight other folk already in their chairs.

I grabbed on to the chair in front of me hard when the whole train jerked, throwing me back.

I ain't saying I squealed or nothing, but I must've sucked in a lot of air, 'cause a girl setting 'crost from me looked o'er and laughed.

It wasn't nothing but the train starting to move.

Looking out the window you'd-a thought the station was moving 'way from us 'stead of the other way 'round. Then afore you know it, we wasn't seeing nothing but trees out the window.

But the strangest thing 'bout it was trying to figger out what it was I was hearing. Even though I ain't never rode a train, what I was hearing was real familiar and sort of comfitting to me.

Then I got it! The train was chugging out my *name* o'er and o'er again!

166

'Twas slow at first, but wasn't no doubt it was saying, "Charl. E. Bo. Bo. Charl. E. Bo. Bo. Charl. E. Bo. Bo."

I looked back at the cap'n to see if he was hearing it too, but he was staring ahead.

The faster the train got a-going, the faster it started calling out to me, "Charl-e-bobo, charl-e-bobo, charl-e-bobo, charl-e-bobo, charl-e-bobo . . ."

Once we got to flying right along and I didn't think the train couldn't go no faster, the sound blurred together same as the trees that was whistling by outside: "CHARLE-BOBO!CHARLEBOBO!CHARLEBOBO!-CHARLEBOBO!"

I thought I was gonna bust, it was so much fun!

I don't know what I done, but all the sudden the cap'n grabbed my collar from behind and says, "Look, you giant hick, it ain't becoming for no one as big and growed-looking as you is to be jumping up and down in his seat and making 'em gigglish goo-goo sounds every time a house go by or some deers look up at you. Try acting your age and pretending you been outta Possum Moan once or twice."

I didn't even blush; a train was 'nough to make anyone get excited.

■ ■ ■ ■

After while, there was something 'bout being on the train that made me want to close my eyes and fall off to sleep. It brung back memories of them times when I was a baby and sleeping would sometimes jus' come up real sneaky and quick and ease all the wakefulness clean outta me.

I ain't for sure if 'twas the way the train rocked steady and gentle from side to side, or if it was the nice, soothish way my name was getting called out again and again, or if it was 'cause of the way the trees and grass and hills was flying by out the window.

If I'd-a thought 'bout it aforehand, I'd-a probably figgered all of that moving going on outside would keep me wide awake, but it was jus' the opposite. Riding on 'em rails so fast meant I couldn't lock my eyes on nothing long 'nough to get a good train of thought going and afore long, falling asleep seemed a better idea than straining my eyes.

The same thing started happening again and again; I'd fight it hard, but I'd find my head nodding up and down on my neck, then I'd give a nervous jerk and wake up, or I'd start dozing till my face smacked up 'gainst the side of the window glass. Each time that happened, there was a greasy face print and a smudge of slobber left on the glass.

I used my fancy shirt sleeve to wipe 'em clean.

I couldn't help thinking this was turrible unfair. Chances was good that this was gonna be the only shot I was gonna get at riding on a train, so falling asleep was jus' 'bout a tragedy.

Everything 'bout being on the train was so beautiful and exciting that I couldn't stand to miss not even one second.

I seent the cap'n had his window open and the air was blowing 'crost him. I axed him to show me how he done it, thinking that the air might help keep me awake, but that was another mistake.

The breeze that come in was warm and cool at the same time and jus' pushed me farther and farther into darkness.

I hate blaming it on something as wonderful as the train, but when I finally falled off to a deep sleep, I falled into the worse nightmare I'd ever had.

For some reason I was out back of our cabin, looking into the forest and still trying to whistle up them three pups that couldn't help theyselfs and had flinched.

There was a heavy fog that was starting to

lift and I was sweeping my eyes 'crost the forest floor, hoping one the pups would show hisself, but all I seent was the trunks of trees coming outta the ground.

A couple of the trunks rooted side by side and standing close together drawed my 'tention 'cause 'stead of being bark, they 'peared to be made outta leather.

My eyes followed the leather tree trunks up and the leather turnt to blue jeans, then the blue jeans turnt into a calico shirt stretched 'crost the wide back of a giant man.

'Twas though I had been cracked by lightning when I rec-a-nized who it was!

"Pap!"

He kept his back to me and said, "Little Charlie, boy, is that you?"

Hearing Pap's voice again near ripped me in half. Happiness and terror was both fighting to smother me. I was torn 'twixt laughing and crying.

He turnt 'round slow and looked at me, but his eyes wasn't his own, they was them same dead eyes I'd seent right after he falled o'er.

This was the first time I 'membered that right after the ax clipped Pap, I'd took a fast-fast look at his face and the wound. I'd cut my eyes 'way quick as I could.

But dreaming eyes don't listen to no one, they look where *they* want for as long's they want; they don't give no considering to what your feelings on the subject is, they don't care a whit what seeing something harsh as this might do to you for the rest of your life.

And my dreaming eyes wanted to study Pap's wound long and hard.

The gash really *didn't* look no different than a big smile. 'Cepting that the white pieces that was where teeth was s'pose to be was broke-up bits of the bones of Pap's forehead that had shattered once that ax-head hit him.

And 'stead of being a set of thin lips, the grinning mouth was really the raggedy edges of the new hole that had got cut in Pap's head. The red thing bulging out of the inside of his mouth that I thought was his tongue wasn't nothing but brain meat oozing from inside Pap's skull.

Then Pap talked.

He said, "Little Charlie, my boy. You's a hunter, boy. Be like them dogs and don't get scairt."

But 'stead of Pap's mouth moving whilst he was talking, the words was falling out of the gash in his forehead. The corners of his new mouth had red slobber stuck to 'em, and the same way the cap'n's brown spit

171

had done, it got stretched up and down with every word Pap said.

My dreaming eyes had had 'nough and looked away. But they wasn't 'bout to give me no shelter from this nightmare.

I turnt my head and seent Ma standing off to Pap's side. Her arms was crossed o'er her chest with her hands holting on to her neck.

She was trying to say something but was having a hard time of it. Her lips was moving but all that was coming out was a gurgling sound.

Ma was getting flus-terated and moved her hands away to reach toward Pap. When she did, I seent there was a long, nasty slash running clean 'crost her throat.

The next thing I knowed, I was getting shook hard and slapped 'crost the back of my head.

I opened my eyes and woke up to the perfect ending of the worst nightmare any person could ever have; 'twas the cap'n standing o'er me with fire in his eyes.

We both screamed for a while afore I shet up and unna-stood what he was saying.

". . . has you lost your mind? Bawling and screaming? You best hesh up. We trying not to draw no 'tention to ourselfs and you's acting like a madman. Now sit up and act growed."

CHAPTER 15

Cat-Hauling

Me and the cap'n went o'er the plan again and again. Mostly he kept finding different ways of letting me know if everything didn't work the way it was s'pose to, it wouldn't be no one's fault but my own.

"Iffen he don't trust you 'nough, then we's through . . ."

"Iffen he ain't drawed to you right off, then we done wasted . . ."

"Iffen you don't do everything I say, we might as well burn a thousand . . ."

"Iffen you don't get him, I'm leaving you here in the land of river rats . . ."

The cap'n acted real mistrusting when he give me the slave woman's necklace he stole off her. He said, "If push come to shove, show him this. It'll let him know we's really here to help."

He capped the whole talk off by saying, "If we was back home, I'd have you cat-hauled if you mess this up."

'Twas cat-hauling that had made Pap so upset and caused him to lose his appetite for two days and his sleep for weeks. I took a chance the cap'n might answer me.

"I don't know what cat-hauling is, sir."

"You'll find out soon 'nough."

One thing I seent 'bout the cap'n, he might be crazy, but he wasn't nowhere near stupid. He'd always listen to what folk had to say, and if they made sense, he'd weigh their words; he wouldn't jus' toss someone's thoughts out 'cause they wasn't agreeing with his.

Maybe the cap'n would tell me 'bout cat-hauling 'cause what good is it to threaten someone with a punishment if they ain't got no idea what the punishment is? What if cat-hauling was something I fount myself enjoying?

"But, Cap'n Buck, sir, ain't you trying to teach me things?"

He didn't answer but looked at me. Listening, thinking.

"I 'preciates you doing it, sir, but how's I s'pose to learn iffen I don't know what you talking 'bout?"

He grunted, then nodded his head once.

"You'll see what cat-hauling is once we gets back home. It's what's gonna happen to the three of them darkies. The boy'll be first, the buck next, and that bigmouth wench last.

"You got to remember darkies is simple, and the best disciplining is always simple. And cat-hauling's 'bout as simple's you can get. You only needs three or four things.

"First, get you a pair a blacksmith gloves; they's the heaviest gloves there is. Then you get someone to go catch holt of the biggest, orneriest, meanest tomcat in the barn. You put the cat in a crate with a lid and have a bucket of cold water at the ready.

"That, a stick, and a hard-head darky's pretty much all you need for a proper cat-hauling. Simple, but it'll make a impression on whoever you's doing it to that's gonna last the rest of their life.

"Many a spirit's been busted after one good cat-hauling, many a darky's eyes has been opened, many a attitude's been changed."

The cap'n wasn't one to do much talking; most times he kept a tight tongue in his head, but once he got the talk ball rolling, he pretty quick started falling in love with the sound of his own words.

"Next you take your darky, strip him nekkid, and stake him on his belly spread-eagled. Then you open the lid of the crate jus' 'nough that you can pour the bucket of water on the cat. Give the crate a good shaking, smack it with the stick once or twice, put them gloves on, open the lid far 'nough that you can reach in and grab the cat by his head. Once you got it gripped good, and believe me, you gonna be surprised how strong one them cats is, grab his tail right at his arse and stretch him out.

"Then you take the kitty to your darky and introduce one to the 'nother. Once they made each other's 'quaintance, you start at the darky's shoulders, haul the tom down the boy's back, then up, then down, jus' like you's using a plane to smooth a big pine board; you ain't gonna be able to tell who's screaming the loudest, the cat or . . ."

My ears jus' up and quit.

I could see the cap'n's lips moving and smiling, I could see the thick drying slobber in the corners of his mouth getting pult north and south, but the only thing I was hearing was the sound of water rushing 'round me.

Even though something inside wasn't letting me hear his words, what he was saying danced 'round in his eyes. They'd started glowing, coming alive, jus' 'bout throwing sparks.

My stomach must be stronger than Pap's, or maybe it was the difference 'twixt being tolt 'bout something and actually seeing it, 'cause whilst what the cap'n was talking 'bout was sickening, I still could've et something.

One thing was for sure, though, I wasn't gonna do nothing else to encourage the cap'n to start talking again.

He said, "You unna-stand, boy? Now you know what cat-hauling is, you satisfied?"

I didn't say nothing.

CHAPTER 16

The Kidnapping of Sylvanus Demarest

Another way them Canadians is different than normal folk is if they fount two trees one next to the other and a patch of grass and some water nearby, they'd turn 'round and call the whole thing a park.

In South Carol-liney, if there was some nice smooth water like this big pond, folks would jus' willy-nilly pull their shoes off and dip their foots in the water, then go home. Or wet a line and pull some fish out.

Not in Canada. Them Canadians are keen on putting benches up and throwing path-ways down so's you could sit and keep a eye on the water and the ducks and gooses. They also put up lots of signs that you didn't even have to know how to read to know what they was saying. They had pictures showing what you wasn't s'pose to do.

179

There was one sign that showed a man holting up a fish on a line with a big X cutting him in parts. Same with a sign showing someone tossing rocks underhand at a bunch of birds in the water with the same X dividing him up, and one that showed a man dropping something with a X. All of 'em had the word *NO* done up in big black letters so's you couldn't make no mistake.

At first I thought them Canadians also done something to the wild gooses and ducks sitting in the water so's they don't tear 'way once you come near 'em the way them down-home birds do.

I figgered they must've tied the birds' legs to something underwater to holt 'em in place, but when I got too close, one 'em big ganders come ripping at me out the water and give me a right proper bite that drawed blood on my leg, which got the cap'n laughing.

I was surprised that all them sitting-in-one-spot ducks and gooses hadn't been took home and cooked. If they was in Possum Moan, all that would be left of 'em would be a feather or two floating on the water and a couple of sets of footprints in the mud showing how far a duck got afore he was snatched up by a barefoot boy.

But maybe these Canadians was doing

something right with this idea 'bout parks, 'cause it sure was soothish and calming to sit there and wait.

We heard the group of young people afore we seent 'em; the cap'n checked his watch and said, "You got to love these folk up north; even the darkies is always on time."

And sure 'nough, it was a bunch of students all dressed up from head to toe, both colored and white. They was chatting and running and jumping 'round with no cares at all.

Once they was 'bout twenty-five, thirty yards from us, I spotted the one who had to be Sylvanus.

My jaw dropped when I seent how big he was. I started wondering right off if he was even bigger than me.

I ain't sure why it was such a surprise; if I'd-a been paying the proper 'tention, I would've knowed that this Sylvanus boy was gonna be big for his age. I mean his pa was purt close to Pap's size and his ma wasn't no shrinking violet of a woman neither. She was the kind of person you wouldn't want to fight less'n you was carrying a good-size stick.

There must've been eight darky boys 'mongst the group of students that come walking toward the pond. I was 'bout as sure as can be the big one was Sylvanus, not jus' 'cause of his size, but 'cause even though everybody knows it's kind of tricky telling one darky from the next, the boy who was a whole head taller than every other student, the one you might've picked out for being the teacher if he wasn't wearing the 'zact same clothes as the other students, and was the one who favored Lou, the woman who was cooling her heels in the Dee-troit jail. If you'd-a put a smock on him and shrunked him down 'bout eight or nine sizes, they was one in the same.

The cap'n said, "I'm thinking it's that one walking by hisself there."

"Why, no, sir, he's the big one. He look the same as his ma."

The cap'n's eyes rolled. "Oh, so you's telling me you can tell one darky from 'nother? Ones that you jus' met?"

"Why, look at him, sir, there ain't no doubt."

I couldn't believe the cap'n didn't see it.

There was something else the cap'n wasn't seeing about Sylvanus neither, and even though the boy was a thief, it had me feeling right sorry and sympathetic for him.

Ma had been poking fun at me once when we was walking home 'cause she said all I'd done that day from when we got to the fields at sunrise to when we left at dusk was ax questions or make comments 'bout Julie Jones.

"Why, Charlie Bobo," Ma had said, "I ain't heard you mention ol' Stanky one time today. That dog's gonna be right jealous you dumped her so easy for something as plain and homely as that skinny, knock-knee Foster girl. You done forgot there's anything else in the world 'cepting for her."

She was right, all I could do was blush, and Ma laughed. "Don't you worry none, Charlie, I felt the same way 'bout your pa first time I seent him cutting trees; I was sure 'nough smited. And once you get smited, ain't nothing you can do 'bout it but hang on for the ride."

Poor ol' Sylvanus had got hisself smited bad! And judging by the way he was skinning and grinning and frolicking 'round this one colored girl, he wasn't holting on for the ride, he was getting dragged foots-first by anything the girl done.

For the first time since I started getting big I could see why the cap'n and Ma would say it ain't becoming for no one big as me to act the way I do sometimes, 'cause when you seent someone as growed-looking as Sylvanus Demarest spooning and mooning o'er this colored gal, it sure didn't look normal, it sure made you take a closer look.

The cap'n said, "We ain't gonna do nothing till tomorrow, but I sure hope you's wrong; it ain't gonna be no picnic getting control of that giant darky."

Then, proving me right, soon as the group of students passed by me and the cap'n's bench, the colored girl slapped at the big boy's arm and said, "Oh, Syl, you are such a tease!"

The cap'n looked at me and swore.

The way Sylvanus's face took a-glowing and the smile he give showed this colored girl could've walked headlong into the middle of the lake and he'd-a sure 'nough followed.

If there wasn't but one drop of human blood in your veins, you couldn't help but feel sorry for the poor sap; we was probably doing him a favor getting him outta this turrible sit-a-way-shun.

We waited for two more days, watching the group of students come and eat and play and have fun with each other. I'd been having such a good time that I was right disappointed when at the end of the second day of sneaking looks at Sylvanus, the cap'n said, "We do it tomorrow."

We'd noticed that after all the other

students would leave, Sylvanus and the colored girl stayed and sat on a bench looking through books. Then after half a hour, the girl would leave and he'd stay another half hour with his nose in a book afore he took off.

"Everything depends on timing," the cap'n tolt me that night, right after Bible reading. "If you do jus' what I tolt you, we can rush the boy out the park right onto the train and have him in Windsor afore his head stops spinning. It ain't no different than running a con; you got to get your mark off balance and keep him that way till it's too late for him to do anything 'cept say, 'Oops!' "

The next day, we got to the park at a quarter to twelve and went to our reg'lar bench.

At 'zactly ten minutes after noon the voices of the students was heard and my stomach started tensing up.

They hadn't paid us one whit of 'tention from day one, but to be on the safe side, the cap'n buried his face in a newspaper and I kept pretending I was looking out at them peculiar-behaving ducks.

Sylvanus and the colored girl was laughing and enjoying one the 'nother's company and I slid my eyes o'er to 'em and something all the sudden hit me and made me want to cry.

It didn't take but a second for me to see that what was grabbing holt of me was what Ma use to call the green-eye monster.

Much as a surprise as it was to me, I was starting to get teary-eye 'cause I was jealous of a darky!

I couldn't help but think, how's this fair? How's it fair that these folk, who was right 'round my age, spent their days reading out of books and laughing and joking and whispering in each other's ears whilst all I done in Possum Moan was have my face looking at the backside of a mule or pulling weeds and working from sunrise to sunset?

How's it fair that they's walking 'round in these fancy u-nee-forms with clean shoes and looking all neat whilst I was most times barefoot in rags?

Ma was right, these darkies *was* living better than white folk.

The cap'n looked at his pocket watch and said, "Wouldn't you know it, she ain't leaving when she s'pose to."

I looked o'er at Sylvanus and the girl; they was both so stuck in their books they must've forgot everything else.

Didn't but a half second go by afore the cap'n looked at his watch again and said,

"If she ain't outta here in a minute, we won't make the train and we's stuck here till next Tuesday. Something tolt me I shouldn't-a bought these tickets."

The cap'n starts up cursing his luck.

I'd been tolt not to do it, but I decided to do something off the top of my head.

Besides, I wanted to see this girl up close.

I walked o'er and rested myself on the bench right next to the girl and Sylvanus.

They was so stuck on 'em books that they didn't take no notice that I was there.

I could unna-stand why Sylvanus was so thunderstrict by the girl; she *was* sort of pretty.

I cleared my throat and said, " 'Scuse me, do y'all know what time it is?"

They both turned their heads up from the books.

She looked at a watch on her arm and said, "Oh, no, Syl! I'm late! It's five minutes after one, sir."

She got up and they shooked hands.

"Hurry along. I shall see you tomorrow, Michelle."

He wouldn't let go of her hand and she laughed.

She said, "Syl!"

She looked at me and said, "Excuse me."

She run off back in the direction they

come from.

Sylvanus give me a smile, then put his head back in his book.

I said, " 'Scuse me again, but ain't you Sylvanus Demarest?"

His mouth falled open and he said, "Pardon me?"

"Ain't you Sylvanus Demarest from Dee-troit, Mitch-again?"

He didn't say nothing, but the look on his face showed he wasn't feeling welcoming to my questions.

"My name is Charlie Bobo and your ma and pa axed me and my uncle to come talk to you. Your ma tolt me it was gonna take some convincing so she said I should tell you that you use to be called Sylvester but now is Sylvanus, that your pa use to be called Cletus but now is Chester, and that she use to be called Lou but is now Eloise. She said since y'all got free, you's changed your name from Tanner to Demarest. She said you'd know the only folks who'd know them things was your ma and pa, and I wouldn't know less'n they tolt me."

The boy was thunderstrict. The cap'n said all we had to do was keep him feeling dizzy for the six-hour train ride and we'd have him in Dee-troit.

I kept talking.

"Your ma and pa need you to come to Dee-troit, Sylvanus. They needs to talk to you face-to-face and they's gotta move fast as they can. They's hiding and need you."

He set the book aside and said, "They're hiding? Is someone hurt? Is something wrong?"

"No, but they needs you soon's possible."

He said, "But why didn't she have Gina write me or even send a wire? Why would she have you —"

"She tolt me to give you something so's you'd know for sure I was here only doing her wishes."

I pult the chain and locket the cap'n had stole offen Sylvanus's ma out of my pocket and swung it back and forth.

Sylvanus rose off the bench and took the chain 'way from me.

He opened the locket, seent the three bundles of hair, and I'll be blanged if tears didn't start coming to his eyes. "Please tell me, I can take it, this is so unusual, something must be very bleak with them. Is Mother or Father badly hurt? For the past month I've had the most horrible premonition! Oh, please forgive me for being so rude earlier! I've been taught not to trust anyone. What did you say your name is?"

The same way being jealous had swept me

up a minute ago, something else swept o'er me now.

It was shame.

I was 'shamed to have to tell this boy, "My name is Charlie Bobo."

This wasn't going to plan at all.

I thought for sure if I could figger a way to get Sylvanus to come 'long with us, the cap'n wouldn't have no choice but to be proud of me and see I wasn't no idiot. I figgered he'd look at me and say, "You done a good job, Little Charlie Bobo."

But when I seent how my lies and tricks had worked so good on this colored boy, the only thing I felt was puny and low.

Only other time I felt near this bad was when I'd come 'crost one of the older boys, Tug Smith, as he was setting a booby trap for Petey the dimwit.

Tug knowed Petey walked home from sweeping a pile of dust from one end of the mill to the other every day. He come by the same way the same time every day.

Tug 'splained to me, "So when he come by, he'll see this here leather pouch laying on the ground and he'll bend o'er to pick it up. Once he do, he'll pull on this string and that'll release this."

Tug pult the string and from the tree on the other side a Bowie knife tied to a piece of cord swung down at the spot where the pouch had been setting.

Tug said, "If I's planned it jus' right, the Tennessee toothpick'll hit Petey right in that fat butt of hisn!"

I seent how dangerous this was and knowed I had to talk Tug out of it.

"Look, Tug, what if that knife hit him in the heart? He could die."

Tug hadn't never thought of that.

I said, "How 'bout 'stead of using the knife, you tie a rock to the end of the rope and aim so's it hits him in the butt? That way it'll jus' bus' him up some, not kill him."

Tug done what I said and I was feeling pretty good 'bout myself for saving Petey.

We hid behind a tree and waited.

Everything went perfect.

Almost.

Petey come by, seent the pouch, bent o'er to pick it up, and the rock come swinging out at him and, 'stead of catching him in the butt, it crashed into his left knee.

There was a loud crack and Petey falled to the ground squealing and holting on to his knee.

Tug bust out laughing so loud I thought he'd bus' his gut.

Petey pult hisself up and acted like he was gonna laugh too, but the pain in his leg was too much and, even though he's got to be more'n thirty years old, he bust out bawling same as a two-year-old.

Tug come from behind the tree and said, "Come on, Petey, be a good sport, it ain't nothing but a joke! It couldn't-a hurt that much, it coulda hurt a lot more."

Petey said, "Shut your mouth, Tug Smith, you ain't nothing but a dirty piece of trash and you ain't never gonna be nothing but dirt for all your days."

Then Petey turnt to me, and even though I hadn't laughed once, he said, "And you, Little Charlie Bobo? I always thought you was my friend! I ain't never done nothing to you!"

His leg give out and he falled back on his butt. Tug near died from laughing. But Petey wasn't done dusting me off.

He said, "I always tolt Ma you treats me good, Little Charlie Bobo, that you wasn't one 'em mean boys! But you is! You's the worse of 'em all 'cause you tricked me into thinking we was friends; you tricked me into thinking you wasn't one 'em laughers. But look at you!"

Petey limped off crying back toward Possum Moan.

I probably should've chased after Petey and 'pologized but I didn't. I swore to myself that I wasn't never gonna do nothing that low-down ever again.

But that same 'zact feeling come creeping up all o'er me when Sylvanus Demarest stood there clutching on to his mother's necklace with tears in his eyes.

My mind run back to that railroad man me and the cap'n come 'crost on the trail that said, even if you get a second chance, all you end up doing is the same thing all o'er again, but in a different place with different folks.

I jus' proved him right.

I was sore confused when the boy reached out his hand and said, "It's a pleasure to make your acquaintance, Charlie Bobo. Please forgive my rudeness."

I hadn't never shook no colored person's hand afore. Didn't seem like a rich white girl's hand could be no softer. I knowed he hadn't done no kind of hard working in his life.

Wasn't no doubt what to do. I had to warn Sylvanus to run and don't stop running till he was away from here. But afore I could say a word, the cap'n butted hisself into our conversation.

I hadn't noticed he'd sat hisself right next to me.

"Yes, son," he said. "Your ma's right worried you wasn't gonna come with us, but she said once you seent her locket you'd know we was here on her bidding. I come 'long with my nephew here to make sure everything go 'cording to plan and we gets you back home safe and sound."

Sylvanus looked from the cap'n to me.

He wiped at his tears and said, "What do I need to do?"

And with them words Sylvanus was ourn.

I could've cried right 'long with him.

Only thing I knowed for sure was I had from 'twixt Saint Catharines and Dee-troit to undo what I done and figger a way to get Sylvanus Demarest away from the cap'n.

We rushed to the train station and got there jus' as a man was calling, "All aboard!"

The cap'n give him three tickets and we clumb up in the train. Me and Sylvanus sat next to each other on the same bench.

The cap'n put hisself di-rect behind us.

He said to Sylvanus, "Could you go ax that conductor when we's s'posed to get to Windsor?"

Sylvanus rose up and said, "Yes, sir."

Soon's he was outta earshot the cap'n says to me, "Keep him talking, don't give him no chance to think on what's happening. You's a natural at this. You done real good so far; keep it up."

I couldn't believe that I'd been looking to curry favor with this man.

When Sylvanus come back, I axed him, "You ever been on a train afore?"

He shook his head.

"Really?"

"No, but it's always been something I've wanted to do."

He looked out the window at the platform and said, "I'd hoped it would be different circumstances than these, though."

I said, "Don't worry, Sylvanus. This all gonna end good."

I thought 'bout his ma and pa in the Deetroit jail and knowed I was lying through my teeth.

He give me a long look and said, "I apologize again. I don't know what I was thinking. Thank you and your uncle for taking the time to come get me; it must be most inconvenient for you. Thank you so much."

He stuck his hand out again and said, "And my friends call me Syl."

I shooked his hand again and said, "Good to meet you, Syl."

The conductor man come through and calls from the front of the car, "Sorry, folks, we expect to be delayed anywhere from forty-five minutes to an hour."

Everyone on the train groaned.

Sylvanus said, "I guess that will give us an opportunity to get to know each other better."

Great.

'Pears that no matter how far you come, how many countries you cross into, the luck of the Bobos follows right along.

CHAPTER 17

Lifting the Wool

I was starting to line up my ducks 'bout the cap'n. More and more 'spicions was getting raised 'bout him every day.

I took a chance to see if Syl could prove something that had been boiling up in me when the cap'n had offered the Dee-troit sheriff all that money to come with us. If he could give the sheriff five hunnert dollars, my and Pap's share should've been more than fifty.

I axed Syl, "So you learnt how to do ciphering in that school?"

He said, "Course I did. I know Latin and Greek too."

Greek?

"What's them, fancy sorts of ciphering like algeeber?"

He give me a look that got my face hot.

"Those are foreign languages."

I didn't care nothing 'bout no foreign language. "But you really can do 'rithmetic?"

"Of course I can."

"I can give you a problem and you can tell me the answer?"

"Try me."

This wasn't gonna be fair; he could give any ol' answer to my question and I got no way of vouching it for true.

What other choice did I have?

"Say I was to sell a dog to a man and I wanted him to pay me one-tenth of what he owed up front; how much did the dog cost to start off?"

Syl give me another blank look and says, "I couldn't tell you."

This wasn't what I was looking to hear, but I probably should've 'spected it. Ma was right, the best these colored folk could do is imitate white people.

I said, "Hmmph, I figgered you couldn't."

He wasn't nothing but a bragging liar.

He tolt me, "I couldn't tell you unless I knew the amount the man had given you at first."

"Say it was fifty whole A-mur-ican dollars."

"I don't even need pencil or paper to

figure that out; all you do with tenths is move the decimal point one place. So if one-tenth of the price of the dog was fifty dollars, the full price would be five hundred dollars.

"Another thing I don't need paper to figure out is that you were planning to rob that man. There aren't any ten dogs that are worth five hundred dollars."

He was saying that only 'cause he didn't know nothing 'bout how spec-tac-a-lar a dog Stanky is, but what really got my goat was that by only giving me fifty dollars, the cap'n was thieving from me, his pard-nah. The least he could've did was to stick a pistol in my face and make it a honest robbery.

Me and Syl couldn't help laughing at the conductor man; he come walking through like he was a machine, saying, "Next stop London, next stop London, next stop London," then he disappeared into the car behind ourn.

I said, "You know what he bring to mind?"

Syl smiled. "What?"

"One 'em automatons, half pocket watch, half tin cup, and half growed man!"

Syl's face brighted up and he laughed so

hard I thought he was gonna cough up a lung!

I said, "I seent the way you look at that colored gal back there; is y'all courting?"

Syl give a big sigh and turned to talk so's no one but me could hear.

"I'm trying; is it that easy to see?"

I smiled.

He groaned. "To tell the truth, I haven't had the courage to talk to her as anything but a friend. She's so beautiful that when I'm set to say something, I lose my nerve. But all the boys want to court Michelle."

He sighed again. "Michelle Taylor. Isn't that a beautiful name?"

I said, "Mine was named Julie Jones. I know jus' what you going through. 'Specially being big as you is and feeling so silly. How tall's you?"

"Six feet and four inches."

"*Naw!* Stand up, that's the same 'zact tallness as me."

We stood up and seent our reflections in the train's window. We *was* the same height!

We both said at the same time, "How much you weigh?"

We laughed and at the same time said, "One hundred and eighty pounds."

Me and Syl was starting to draw dirty

looks from the cap'n, so we got back in our chairs.

When the train give a jerk and stopped in London, the man who was sitting 'crost the way from us got off.

Jus' as the man walked by us, the cap'n leant forward and tolt me and Syl, "Y'all quit all that folderol and act like you got some sense."

The man turned his head quick and with hot eyes kept looking from me and Syl to the cap'n.

He was fixing to say something, but the fancy automaton conductor standing at the door said, "Sir? We're trying to make up time."

The man turned and got off the train.

I must be catching the cap'n's seventh sense, 'cause something 'bout the way the man looked at us left me feeling unsettled and itchy.

I looked back at the cap'n to see if he'd caught the itching too, but he was staring ahead.

It must be my conscience plaguing me.

I looked out the window and the man walked fast-fast to a colored woman who was standing in the station door.

He said something to her and was pointing o'er at the car we was in.

The conductor flipped the steps up and yelled, "All aboard," as the woman come running toward the train.

The locomotive started calling me slow, "Charl. E. Bo. Bo. Charl. E. Bo. Bo. Charl. E. Bo. Bo."

The woman run next to where we was setting. She jumped up to get herself a good look.

The engine picked up speed. "Charl. E. Bobo. Charl. E. Bobo. Charl. E. Bobo. Charl. E. Bobo. Charl E. Bobo."

The woman turnt 'round waving at the man on the platform as though she'd lost her mind.

Judging by the way she was nodding her head up and down and moving her lips, it was plain she was screaming, "Yes! Yes! Yes!"

"CHARLEBOBOCHARLEBOBOCHARLEBOBOCHARLEBOBO."

It didn't matter what them two was so worked up 'bout, I knowed it was too late and they couldn't do nothing to stop us. My heart sunked when I knowed we was in the cap'n's grip and wasn't nothing that could be done.

"Next stop Chatham, next stop Chatham, next stop Chatham."

The conductor walked 'tween the seats.

The cap'n axed the automaton, "How long to Windsor?"

"After we leave Chatham, there's one stop five minutes later in Buxton, then another forty-five minutes to Windsor. Probably pretty close to an hour, Sir."

The cap'n give a big sigh and smile and said to Syl, "Well, boy, won't be long now 'fore you see your ma; ain't that grand?"

Syl returned the smile and said, "I can hardly believe it, sir."

"What 'bout you, Little Charlie? Can you believe it?"

He couldn't-a cut me no deeper if he'd used Jim Bowie's own Tennessee toothpick.

He leant back in his seat, crossed his hands behind his head, closed his eyes, and said, "Struck dumb, huh, Little Charlie? I knows how you feels, I caint believe it neither. There's gonna be some real cellybrating once we reach Dee-troit."

The cat had bit something on the mouse hard 'nough that it couldn't run no more and all I could do was look down at my hands in my lap, knowing I was doing jus' as much biting as this low-down cap'n.

Syl said, "What's wrong, Charlie?"

I shook my head and looked out the window as we pulled into the Chat-ham train station.

I'd figgered things wrong when I said afore that tricking Syl was as bad as what I done to Petey with the rock and rope. I knowed now they wasn't even close; this was it. Helping get Syl put in Mr. Tanner's hands was the most 'shamed I'd ever feel 'bout anything in my life.

Any chance I'd had of warning Syl now was long gone; the cap'n wasn't 'bout to let him outta his sight till he was shackled in Dee-troit.

❧ CHAPTER 18 ❧

Folk in Canada Ain't Right

The conductor yelled, "Chatham," opened the door at the front of the car, and pushed the big set of steps down to the platform.

The cap'n looked out of his window and give a snort.

He leant up to me and whispered, "Well, if this don't beat all! Look at what's getting on the train; it's a go-rilla wearing a twenty-five-dollar suit!"

A short, dark-skin colored man in a fancy suit and round-topped hat walked up the stairs into the train.

He looked 'round the mostly empty car afore he took a chair jus' the other side of the lane from me and Syl.

Syl leant forward on our bench and said, "Afternoon, sir."

The colored man smiled and nodded at Syl.

Sitting behind us, I could feel the wind was getting into the cap'n's sails and he was 'bout to raise Cain that a darky thought he could set hisself next to white folk without axing first.

But the fancy-dressed colored man snatched the wind outta *everyone*'s sails when he said clear out the blue, "Are you having a pleasant trip, Sylvanus?"

Me and Syl both was shocked.

"Why, yes, sir. How do you know my name, sir?"

Cap'n Buck's seventh sense kicked in; he said, "Call that little go-rilla 'sir' one more time and I'll have you wishing you wasn't born."

Syl looked back at the cap'n and the surprised face he made showed he was really seeing him for the first time.

The cap'n leant toward the man and said, "Now look here, boy, you best tell me how you know this darky's name and I don't mean maybe."

The short man laughed and said, "Really? You're quite the big bug, aren't you, little fella?"

The cap'n was tongue-tied! Didn't no *white* folk dare talk to him with that kind of tone down in South Carol-liney, and this colored man had the nerve?

The mouthy man said, "If you look out of that window, you'll see there's a welcoming committee gathering in your honor, and it's growing by the minute."

Even though the cap'n couldn't pull his eyes offen this dark man, I couldn't help myself; I looked out the window.

He was right! There must've been thirty colored folk — men, women, boys, and girls, some of 'em holting on to sticks and guns. There wasn't one happy face 'mongst the whole boodle of 'em and all their 'tention was pointed in the di-rection of the car we was in.

There was another ten or fifteen white folk with guns, sticks, and scowls too. And the peculiar thing was, 'stead of attacking the colored ones, they was mingling right 'longside of 'em!

The black man in the fancy duds said, "I represent the Chatham-Buxton Vigilance Committee. To be more accurate, I repre-sent the decent, law-abiding faction of the committee. They" — he ducked his head toward the windows — "do not. Now, which of us would you prefer dealing with, shorty?"

It took him a while to get his footing, but

the cap'n wasn't 'bout to be bluffed down.

He spluttered out, "Why . . . I . . . I *demand* you let me go 'bout doing my legal duty! You think I ain't run into no uppity darkies afore? I promise you, you gonna rue this day if you don't let us be."

The man said, "Suit yourself."

He stuck out his hand toward Syl.

"Sylvanus, please come with me."

Syl was confused. He looked from the man to me, then said, "But, sir, my mother has sent Charlie and his uncle to fetch me to Detroit."

I felt my face growing hot.

The man said, "Sylvanus, these men are not your friends."

"But —"

The man barked, "Boy! It jus' isn't right that someone as large and as advanced at school as you can be so gullible. If you do not get your no-common-sense, naïve, foolish arse out of that seat this minute, I'll *really* make you wish you'd never been born."

Afore Syl could move, the cap'n snatched his throat from behind with his left hand, then reached his right hand into his pocket. When it come out, it was gripped 'round his six-shooter.

He mashed the barrel of the pistol into the side of Syl's head and tolt the man,

"There's jus' one of two ways this darky's getting off this train.

"The first is y'all can walk off together, holting hands, singing and skipping, for all I care. But that ain't happening till somebody's give back the one thousand five hunnert A-mur-ican dollars this boy's ma and pa stole from his master.

"The second way is someone's gonna have to carry him and you both off, and they best brang a pail and a mop for cleaning brains off the floor iffen you don't yield, boy."

The black man put his hands up and backed away.

"Don't do anything you'll regret."

"Shet your mouth, you uppity little Sambo. You telling a white man what to do? What kind of place is this?"

I couldn't believe the way the cap'n was almost whining when he said, "Ain't there even no white man I can talk to?"

The fancy-dressed colored man eased toward the train's door, then disappeared down the steps.

The cap'n said, "What'd he think he was gonna do, come up on this train and waltz off with this darky jus' 'cause he said so? I ain't never backed down from no darky in South Carol-liney and I ain't 'bout to start that bad habit jus' 'cause I come 'crost some blanged border.

"I know now what that Dee-troit sheriff meant when he said this was something you have to see to believe! Hearing them words come out that go-rilla's mouth all proper and fancy-sounding wasn't no stranger than if a murder of crows got together and started up singing 'Amazin' Grace'!"

Poor Syl! He hadn't moved since the cap'n snatched his neck.

He kept his eyes clenched tight and his hands was holting on to the cap'n's left hand, which was wrapped 'round his throat. He had the look 'bout him of one 'em kittens whose mother had bit holt of the scruff of its neck and was walking 'round with it swaying from one side to the 'nother.

The cap'n said, "So far, you done good, Little Charlie; you standing tall and keeping your trap shet. Lots of boys your age couldn't-a done that. You's gonna make a fine overseer. I'm gonna —"

The train lurched, throwing me back into my seat.

I could hear my name being called slow. "Charl. E. Bo. Bo. Charl. E. Bo. Bo. Charl. E. Bo. Bo."

But the sound faded away from us and after that first jerk, the train hadn't moved a bit.

The cap'n dragged Syl back to his seat, then o'er to one of the train's windows. He forced Syl's head out, then jammed the gun's barrel in his ear.

Keeping his head di-rect behind Syl's, he yelled, "What was that? What y'all up to? If someone don't talk, I swear that platform's gonna be running with this boy's blood."

A white man spoke up. "The locomotive has been disconnected from the train, sir."

"*What?* You best tell him he's got three minutes to hook it back up and get us to Windsor."

"Well, sir, that train's already left the station."

The cap'n took the Lord's name in vain.

The man said, "I'm Sheriff Geoffrey Sudbury, sir. I'm certain I can help get you safely out of this and back on your way to the United States. But if we're to talk, you simply must remove that pistol from the young man's head."

The cap'n said, "You's the sheriff? Well, sir, upholt the law! This boy's a fugitive and he's under my legal arrest. I demand you do your God-give duty and banish this mob, hook that locomotive back up, and let us pass!"

The cap'n let go of Syl's neck and fumbled 'round till he got his slave-hunting badge outta his pocket. He helt it in front of Syl's face.

"This here says I'm a legal agent of the U-nited States of A-mur-ica. Y'all don't want to get me riled."

The sheriff said, "Sir, we're Canadians; riling people isn't in our nature. But perhaps you failed to notice you're no longer in the United States. With that in mind, if there's to be any more conversation, I insist you take the firearm off of this young man and hand it to me."

"Are you daft?" The cap'n pointed at me and tolt the man, "The minute I take this pistol offen this boy, them darkies will rush the train and tear me and my son to shreds."

His son!

His *son*? I near swore out loud when the cap'n hooked me to his family that way.

The Canadian sheriff said, "My good man, if you do not immediately desist threatening that child, we won't be able to discuss anything. Now, please, hand me the pistol."

The cap'n said, "I swears on a whole tower of Bibles that ain't never gonna happen."

He pulled Syl's head from out the window and, putting the cat-neck grip back on him, scooted with him toward the lane that run 'twixt the seats. I could see the cap'n had pressed the gun so hard 'gainst Syl's ear that a line of blood was running down the right-hand side of his face.

He said to me, "All right, Little Charlie Bobo, we's in a real pickle here, but if you do everything I says, we gonna be in Dee-troit in time for supper, laughing 'bout this."

He tapped the gun on Syl's head and said, "And you gonna be where you wished you was, in your mammy's arms picking cotton in South Carol-liney 'stead of strutting 'round Canada pretending you's white. Big as you is, you's a three-thousand-dollar darky if ever there was one."

He said to me, "I promises you, Little Charlie, you do everything I says and we'll be fine. You hear me?"

"Yes, sir."

We felt the train rock toward the station side of the tracks.

I said, "They hooked the train back up!"

The cap'n closed his eyes for a second, then said, "They ain't hooked nothing; there's a gang of men boarding the train on them cars in front and behind. They gonna come at us from both ends."

He let out a puff and said, "All right. This is it, lads. Both of y'all do 'zactly as I says or we's all gonna die right here."

He pushed Syl into the lane and followed behind.

He steered Syl down onto the top step of the train, then fast-fast squozed up behind him. He bobbed his head from side to side. I figger that's so's no one could get a clean shot at him without taking a chance on hitting Syl.

"Follow close behind, Little Charlie."

The crowd falled back, but they wasn't so far back that we couldn't hear the gasps and moans they made once they seent the sit-a-way-shun.

The cap'n yells so's everyone can hear him, "My son's armed too, and even if none of y'all's heard of me, I knows you heard of him.

"That's right, this here's Baby Face Bobo. Young as he look, he done tracked down sixteen runaway slaves by hisself. Only had to kill two of 'em in the process. Y'all don't wanna mess with him. Y'all might get us, but at least twelve a you's gonna be escorting us to damnation."

At first I thought the cap'n was making me a part of his family so's to bluff these people, but then I seent he wasn't doing nothing but tying our fates together, making it so no one could see me for what I really am, a young innocent boy 'stead of

214

being a child of the devil.

With them words, the cap'n had jus' writ my funeral speech.

He yells back at me, "Baby Face, stay close, but I'm begging you, don't start killing no one jus' yet."

I was a goner.

I helt the gun at my side and stepped behind the cap'n and Sylvanus.

More grumbling come from the crowd.

The cap'n whispered, "Holt that gun up, boy."

I didn't move.

He hissed at me, "The first shot's going into your playmate here and the second's yourn less'n you holt that gun up."

I raised the pistol so's everyone could see it.

More sighs and sharp drawing-ins of breath come from the crowd.

The three of us moved real slow. We was bunched up so tight and moving so jerky and clumsy we must've looked like a hunnert-year-old man with six legs.

Finally, the cap'n reached the last of the steps and let Syl drop onto the platform. He stepped off behind him.

The cap'n yelled, "Sheriff, I wants three horses, which I'll leave at the ferry in Windsor. If I don't get 'em, this boy is dead.

Y'all got five minutes and the clock is running. I ain't to be trifled with."

The sheriff took a couple of steps toward us with his hands helt up. But afore he could say a word, a old, dried-up colored woman hollered out, "Oh, my Lord! No! No! No! It caint be!"

She raised her hand, pointing a shaking, crooked black finger in our direction.

"I knows this devil! I knows him! He done cleant hisself up, but I knows that voice! I done heard that voice every night in my sleep for nine year. You's Massa Tanner's man, Cap'n Buck!"

She walks slow from the crowd and her mouth was tore wide open. Things was moving so peculiar that I can't say if she was screaming or not, but it ain't really important; the look on her face was 'nough to make every hair on my body stand up like porky-pine quills.

She was pulling on her hair so hard her eyebrows was halfway up her forehead.

"Has you forgot me, Mr. Cap'n? Sir?"

Her body and face was twisted to make you think demons had grabbed holt of her.

"Do you remember my girl? Did you even know her name? She was Rose O'Sharon. Do you hear me? Rose O'Sharon was her name. Has you forgot?"

She tried screaming the girl's name again, but the words ripped her throat apart.

The cap'n turned to look at the woman . . .

Things started in moving *real* slow, giving me plenty of time to think good and clear.

I *could* say what happened next happened 'cause I'd done a whole lot of pondering on it, or it was something I'd been waiting on, waiting for the 'zact right minute to do, but them would be lies.

I really done it 'cause of that man who use to work on the railroad. His words had got blowed so deep under my skin that only way they'd come out was when the worms reclaimt 'em.

I wasn't 'bout to make the same mistake once 'gain. I wasn't 'bout to make however much time I had left living be a slow-moving train wreck. I knowed the cap'n was evil 'nough to pull this off and get us all to Dee-troit. I knowed Sylvanus and his ma and pa was gonna be slaves 'gain. And I knowed it would be my doings that caused it.

I 'membered everything Pap tolt me 'bout shooting and looked in the pistol's cylinders to check the bullets.

My heart dropped into my gut.

The cap'n didn't trust me 'nough to give

me a loaded gun. The chambers was all empty.

I 'membered when I first met the cap'n and how I thought I outweighed him by eighty pounds and could real easy smash his head in with my fist. I hadn't lost no weight since then; fact is, we'd been eating so good up in Dee-troit and Canada I'd probably put on another ten, fifteen pound.

And I was thinking 'bout Pap and how the cap'n had made it so that he was tore up by nightmares from watching a baby get cat-hauled.

A baby.

I knowed after the next minute I was either gonna be a dead boy or someone riding to Windsor with a broke-up heart.

The last straw that busted the wagon's axle was when something the cap'n had said in the moonlight in the river finally made itself clear to me. It was only one word and it exploded in my head like a boiler.

He'd called me "orphan."

I swung my right fist as hard as I could, aiming at the cap'n's face.

Time was slow 'nough that I seent his nose flatten out and spread o'er his cheeks, looking like someone had slapped him in the face with a piece of brownish Georgia ham.

I felt bones crunching and wasn't for sure if they was his or mine.

It didn't really matter; the cap'n's eyes rolled back in his head, and he turnt Syl a-loose and staggered a bit. Syl fell to his knees jus' in front of the cap'n and started struggling to get holt of his breath.

I'd mis-underestimated how hard-head the cap'n was. I'd just stunned him for a second; I hadn't knocked him down at all.

The cap'n turnt to me and his eyes was aglow with something past hating.

He said, "It figgers. I should've give you the same treatment I give your ma. And after all I done for you . . ."

He raised the pistol and leveled it at my head.

Syl pushed the cap'n's arm up right as he fired. The bullet whistled o'er my head and smacked itself into the train, shattering glass.

Then, the cap'n had been right, the mob was on us.

Syl got crowded up on by a bunch of folk and shoved and pushed and pulled till the last I seent of him, he was disappearing through the door of the train station.

The cap'n's squeal was the same as a pig that was on the wrong end of a dull knife.

Then there was a swarming done by the

fanciest-dressed colored folk that ever come together, piling into the spot where I was. I felt a hunnert different hands, black and brown 'long with a good sprinkling of white ones, snatching and tugging and poking and grabbing at every part of me.

Then, doggone it all, time *really* slowed down, letting me ponder my pruh-dic-a-mint.

If someone was to ax me aforehand, I'd-a said I couldn't think of nothing worst than getting jumped on by a whole vexed mob.

But it didn't take long to see that laying a good beating on someone is problemish for a mob once they decide that's what they gonna do.

First off, everyone's too squozed up, one atop the 'nother; there ain't near 'nough space for no one to throw a proper punch. Soon's someone rears back to slug you, their elbow's bound to bump into someone else that's looking to snatch hair out your head and most the power gets sapped out the punch.

Second off, and I ain't for sure this happens in every mob beating, but in mine they was too excited and worked up to really do the damage they could've did if they jus' calmed down some. They was willy-nilly throwing punches and kicks and swinging sticks and wasn't hitting me with but one or so blows outta ten.

Why, they bloodied one the 'nother's noses jus' as good as they bloodied mine! I knowed it wasn't me what got no good licks in, 'cause I didn't throw one punch. The farthest thing from my mind was hitting someone; I jus' wanted to roll up in a ball and get left alone.

Even though my lip got busted pretty good, I got through the trouble with all my teeth still setting in the proper spots in my jaw, but I seent one colored man lose a front tooth to a vicious left cross that missed me by two whole foots!

But one peculiar thing a mob *can* do that I ain't never seent happen when you's getting whupped by one person, or even three, is to beat you clean out your clothes. Which was a real tragedy 'cause these was the first and only set of new clothes I 'spect I'll ever get in my life.

Jacket, necktie, shirt, britches, shoes, socks, all of 'em got snatched and ripped to rags and floated off somewhere. Each time someone connected with a punch and drawed back their fist, a bit of my brand-new, store-bought clothes was gripped up in their fingers. I s'pose if I was wearing unmentionables, they'd-a got beat off me too.

But the Lord works in mysterious ways; it was two of the oddest things that come together and saved my life. And believe it or not, the first was getting beat nekkid.

The second is the man the cap'n called a suit-wearing go-rilla.

Once them folk beat my clothes offen me, 'twas that man that throwed hisself into the crowd and kept 'em from finishing me off.

"What is wrong with you? Stop! Stop this instant! This is nothing but a young boy," he screamed. "Can't you see the only hair he's got is on his head!"

I looked down and was so flat-out embarrassed that I was grateful when a colored man who had big blacksmith arms was patient 'nough to take careful aim with his punch and knock me cold!

CHAPTER 19

Dee-troit, One Week Later

The pain near kilt me, but I pushed open the heavy door to the Dee-troit jail.

I guess it could be said I helped Syl get free of the cap'n, but there was more I had to do.

The sheriff barely looked at me afore he dropped his nose back in the newspaper. Keegan coughed and spit.

"Well, I stands corrected," the sheriff said. "I didn't think I'd be seeing anything of y'all again."

"Well, sir, I didn't think we was gonna make it back neither. 'Twas turrible right from the minute we set foots in Canada."

The Dee-troit sheriff said, "Don't say I didn't warn y'all.

"Your pard-nah outside?"

He set his reading specs aside and looked

at me for the first time.

"And what in sweet baby Jesus's name happened to you? You sure ain't no kid no more. You musta been dragged 'twixt Toron-o and here behind a hoss."

"Well, sir, *that* ain't what happened, but I 'spect the feeling of that ain't much different than what did go on."

"Do tell, youngster, do tell."

"Do you mind if I sit, sir? I'm still aching near everywhere."

"Go 'head, boy." He pointed at a chair. "How'd you get to be in such a state?"

I eased myself down in the chair, but it didn't help much; even my rear end was hurting.

Once I got my breathing back, I said, "We run the boy down in a town called Saint Catharines and got him into the train with us. We brung him with no problems down to this horrible city by name of Chat-ham.

"The train stops and a crowd of the best-dressed colored folk you ever seent carrying sticks and waving guns gathers up and say we got to give the boy back. Well, once I seent the odds we was bucking up 'gainst, I was all for letting him go, but the cap'n seent things different, says he ain't standing for that at all, said he ain't never backed down from no darkies in A-mur-ica and wasn't 'bout to start the bad habit of doing it in Canada.

"The cap'n was a man of his word too; wouldn't back down from a crowd of two, three hunnert yelling and screaming colored folk. Dared 'em to do anything to him."

"You don't say? Did they listen to him?"

"I think some of 'em must've, 'cause once they commenced tearing him apart, it do seem a good bit of 'em jus' stood to the side cheering folk on and didn't join in.

"But them that did, ooh-ooh-ooh-wee! They didn't give him one ne'er-you-mind; they was busting to take him up on his dare. Last I seent of him, he was bloodied and buck-nekkid at the foots of a crowd of near a thousand colored folk and pre-turbed white folk too.

"Syl . . . the runaway boy we near caught . . . got clean away."

The Dee-troit sheriff says, "Well, if they was so set on killing y'all, what you doing here?"

Telling 'bout getting beat so bad you ended up buck-nekkid was too embarrassing. Like Pap use to say, "Sometimes a good lie can smooth the roughest road for folk."

I tried to smooth the road for both me and the sheriff. "I can't really say for sure, sir. Seems I was already knocked 'way from my senses when they choosed if they was gonna let me go.

"When I come to, first thing I notice is that every bit of me from head to toe is sore and achy like it ain't never been afore. I fount out even your eyelashes can be a-throbbing.

"Then I sees I'm sitting in a jail cell with the door wide open. I ain't never been in no jail afore, but I figgered one the points of being in one is that the door is always s'pose to be locked on you.

"That's a right peculiar way to wake up, so I'm waiting to see if I can remember how I got there. 'Bout that time the Chat-ham sheriff come in and welcomes me back to being awoke.

"I axed him how long I'd been out and he says nigh on five days.

"I axed him what happened to the cap'n and he looked kind of nervous and said, 'I'd rather not discuss that at this moment.' "

Something else I wasn't gonna tell Sheriff Turner was how ha-miliating it was when I noticed I was wearing the biggest set of diapers you ever seent.

I said to Sheriff Turner, "I tried getting off the cot I'm laying in and that's when I seent my left foot's all bandaged up and too sore to walk on.

"The Chat-ham sheriff tells me my little toe on my left foot was so chawed up that the doctor had to cut it offen me. Tolt me it was done by a colored doctor too!

"But that ain't the bad news you'd think it is; now whenever I goes barefoot, I'll look down and get a good reminder of my pap! He lost two of his toes and I jus' lost one, but that do give us something in common.

"So I leans back on the cot and wait to see what part of me was gonna quit hurting first.

"Truth tolt, I starts getting com-fitted jus' laying 'round. It give me lots of time to think 'bout what I was gonna do next."

The sheriff said, "So what you come up with?"

There was one other thing I sure wasn't 'bout to tell these two. Whilst me and the Chat-ham sheriff was waiting on the train to take me back to Windsor, he'd handed me the old wore-out rucksack he'd been carrying.

I'd tolt him, "Thank you, sir. What's this for?"

The Chat-ham sheriff set off looking discom-fitted again.

He started up blinking like there's salt in his eyes and said, "Young man, some of the time in the heat of the moment things happen that aren't exactly intended. The contents of that bag are simply the remains of one such occurrence. Please check to make certain everything's there."

I squatted down and set the rucksack on the floor of the train station.

Soon's I opened it a familiar stank chawed at my nose. The cap'n's hat was atop of everything. I took it out and set it on the floor. Underneath the hat was the cap'n's good suit of clothes. Or what was left of 'em. Under that was a boot, a belt, and a shrunked-down Bible.

Banging 'bout at the bottom of the bag was the slave-hunting badge and the cap'n's six-shooter.

I looked at the sheriff. I didn't know what to say.

He tolt me, "We know you say the two of you weren't related, but perhaps you could see these are returned to his family."

I was grateful the sheriff had took me out the cap'n's family, but I didn't want nothing to do with his garbage.

"Sir, that's kind of you, but I don't know none his kin."

I gripped the cap'n's gun by the barrel and reached it toward the sheriff.

"Could you take this and I'll toss the rest

in the trash?"

He said, "Well, I'll take the gun but only to dispose of it. I'll see that all of his goods are thrown out."

He started blinking again when he said, "While the people here may have a tendency to become a bit overwrought and inappropriately enthusiastic concerning some matters, son, none of them are thieves."

His hand went in his jacket and come out with a envelope and the cap'n's wallet.

He handed me the envelope and said, "This is fifty dollars American, which we calculate would more than cover the cost of the gentleman's boots and suit."

I tolt him, "Thank you kindly, sir, but he wouldn't-a done nothing but wore that suit of clothes till it was stiff as wood anyway. Seems to me if I was 'em clothes I'd be a lot happier to get put out my misery quick than to have to die slow and stanking on the cap'n's back. Don't no one owe nothing for them things."

He wouldn't take the money back and handed me the cap'n's wallet.

"We found it contained five-hundred-and-forty-one dollars American. Please count to make certain it's all there."

My hands set to shaking as I opened the wallet and looked at all the money the cap'n was toting. I wished I knew ciphering as good as Sylvanus so's I could count it out proper.

I tolt him, "Do I have to count it, sir, or can I just take your word?"

He smiled. "Put it away, young man, and be careful."

"Cat got your tongue, boy?" Sheriff Turner said loudly. "What you come up with?"

I tolt him part of what I knowed I had to do.

"I'm taking 'em two slaves you's holting for us back to South Carol-liney by myself."

Him and Keegan 'changed a look.

"I'm telling you that's a even worse idee than y'all going to Canada was.

"You ain't never gonna make it. You ain't got no pard-nah, you ain't even got no dog. It'd be hard 'nough if you was jus' toting one runaway back, but two? My, my, my, that's a tall order even for someone who's seasoned as your friend the cap'n is . . . or was, whatever the case may be."

"What choice I got, sir?"

"What choice? How 'bout you chooses staying alive? How 'bout you chooses to send a wire to tell 'em folk back home to send you some help?"

"There ain't no one can come, sir."

He reached his hand out for me to shake

230

it. I did. Every finger throbbed when he turnt my hand loose.

"Boy, I hopes you enjoyed your brief time on the earth, 'cause it coming to a end a lot sooner than you think."

Keegan said, "What kinda bounty is y'all 'specting to get for them two?"

Soon as I said it, I knowed I shouldn't-a. " 'Round 'bout two, three thousand dollar."

Keegan whistled one long note.

"That'll set up a man for a good long time, won't it, Sheriff Turner? Yes, sir, a whole lot of com-fitting can be got outta that!"

The sheriff said, "You sure I caint talk you outta this?"

"No, sir, there ain't nothing else I can do."

"Well, I'm 'vising 'gainst it again, but let's get your folks ready."

The sheriff took me to where the woman was sharing a cell with four other colored gals and two white ones.

The sound of us coming in had all their heads perked up looking worrifully at the cell door. The only one who wasn't paying us no mind was Syl's ma. She was squatted down in a corner with her hands holting on to her face.

The six other women's heads all dropped soon's they seent we didn't have no business with them.

The sheriff said, "All right, gal. Your carriage awaits. You 'bout to go home; come on."

She didn't move.

"Wench, don't make me come in that cell."

The woman got up slow.

She come to the cell's door, studied my face a bit, then says, "Ain't you the one that went to Canada with the cap'n?"

I nodded my head. It wasn't a good idea; one the cords in my neck tightened up and made me give a cry.

"Where my boy at?"

"I don't know. Last I seent of him, a crowd stole him from us and rushed him off."

"What kind of crowd?"

" 'Twas about a thousand colored folk with sticks and guns with a hunnert or so white ones mixed in 'mongst 'em."

Why, I got to tell you the look that come o'er that woman's face sure wasn't what you'd 'spect to see from no one that knowed they was a week or two away from a good hiding afore they went back to picking cotton in the hot sun all day. You'd-a thought I tolt her I was gonna split the reward money with her. She jus' 'bout stumbled.

One of the other colored women said, "Child, we's so happy for you!"

They hugged each other and patted one the 'nother's backs whilst smiling hard and whispering.

The sheriff tolt 'em to break it up and hustled Syl's ma out the cell, through the door to the holting room.

Soon's she was out, Sheriff Turner said to me, "Where's your shackles at?"

I showed him what we'd brung.

He looked at 'em and said, "These ain't no good for what you planning on doing. You need traveling shackles. I got some you can buy cheap."

The sheriff pointed at the bench and tolt Syl's ma, "You set right there till we come back with them chains, gal."

He went through another door, leaving me and the woman alone.

She said, "My boy, sir, you talk to him?"

"Yup."

"He look OK? What he say?"

I looked at the door where the sheriff was shackling her husband.

I tolt her, "Well, I gotta say if you and him didn't favor one the 'nother so much, I wouldn't never thought you give birth to him. You talks normal, but that boy a yourn been keeping his nose in a schoolbook so much he's started talking like one. You'd be embarrassed to death if you was to see the airs he's putting on. And other than them Tanners, he dressed better than any white folk I'd seent in South Carol-liney!

"You'd weep tears of shame if you was to see the way Syl's carrying on."

I wasn't looking to pile on the agony for Syl's ma, but the truth's the truth.

Keegan come in and hefted the shackles o'er to her. She looked up and, smiling to beat the band and with her black face a-shining with tears, she stood up and raises her hands out front of her, as though she's 'specting him to give her a big piece of chocolate cake with mint icing 'stead of the chains he was fixing to.

Keegan said to her, "Gal, has living up north all these years made you lose your mind? Has you gone so daft you's forgot what's a-waiting on you down in South Carol-liney? Ain't no one playing no game with you."

She talked to him bold as any white man would.

"You listen here, if this was a game, I done won it nine time o'er!"

He laughed at her and said, "What you

won? You 'bout to go back to being a slave. You ain't gonna have nothing."

"What I won? Lemme tell you, mista man. I done give birth to twin girls that you or that stanking cap'n or n'en one n'em other savages Massa Tanner gonna send up here ain't never gonna find no matter how hard y'all looks.

"And our Sylvanus! Our baby boy! Who even this gigantic white boy, wit' his sorry, trashy self, say is talking proper and dressing good as a prince and doing jus' fine, and writing us letters in his own hand! And judging by the way the both of y'all looks and talks, them's things neither one of y'all can't even dream 'bout doing."

I started up blushing hard.

But she wasn't done.

She spread her fingers on her right hand and helt it in Keegan's face. Starting with her thumb, she commenced counting down, rolling each finger one at a time into her palm as she talked.

"What I won? I was owned by them Tanners, my ma was owned by them Tanners, her ma was owned by them Tanners, her ma was owned by them Tanners, and her ma afore that too."

After reciting all her mas and grandmas that was owned by the Tanners, her hand was balled in a hard black fist.

With her palm pointing up, she all the sudden throwed her fingers open like she been holting on to a hand full of something, dust maybe.

Then she blowed into her hand and gusts it all away.

She said, "But that done come to a end with my girls! They ain't owned by no one, they's free! Them and Sylvanus is free!

"Oh, yeah, them Tanners might have holt o' me and Chester now, but see if we do one minute of work again.

"Chester know, I know, and them Tanners know what gonna have to be done with us. But no matter how slow and drawed-out they make the end for us, they ain't getting one second of them nine years and six months back. Not one second.

"What I won? I'm-a go to my grave knowing my chirren is free, and me and Chester gonna be going home too. That's what I won.

"My girls is in Buxton! *Buxton!*

"You know what that mean? It mean you'd have better luck going into hell and snatching a poke chop off the devil's own dinner plate than you'd have of getting them babies back to the Tanners."

The sheriff come in and said, "Keegan,

why you looking to get her all worked up? Let's jus' get 'em shackled proper and out on the road."

The sheriff took me to a third door in the holting area. There was a big crate up 'gainst the wall.

"Why, sir, I already got shackles. I don't see no need to buy other ones."

"Let me ax you, boy. Once you get out in the woods with them darkies, what on God's green earth is gonna stop that buck from pulling you offen that horse and skinning you alive?"

"I'm fully armed, sir."

"What difference do that make? I'm telling you all they gonna do is wait for the right second to jump you. And 'em light shackles will jus' give him something to strangle the life outta you. Only thing that can prevent that is these."

He pulled the heavy wood crate into the holting room.

It didn't take long for me to see the difference 'tween my shackles and the ones the sheriff wanted me to use.

It was the difference 'twixt a puny two-day-old calf and a prize thousand-and-a-half-pound bull.

One was skinny and stringy and the other'n was all thick muscles and solid bone. With twenty years of good eating, my shackles might grow up to be half the size of the sheriff's. One meant business and the other'n didn't.

There was also a four-foot-long iron bar that had a thick metal U welded on each end. There was holes cut in each end of the U. It musta weighed sixty pounds.

At the bottom of the crate was iron staples and bolts and yards and yards of thick, heavy chains.

The sheriff said, "Keegan, put the crate on the wagon, and soon's you ready, boy, you and me'll head on o'er to the blacksmith to get these darkies locked down proper."

It wasn't but a short trip to the black-smith's.

The sheriff said, "Hello, Dale. I brung you some irons that needs to be closed down on some runaways."

The blacksmith said, "Afternoon, gennel-men. How many you need bolted in?"

"Jus' the two of 'em, thank you kindly, Dale." The sheriff smiled. "This boy's tak-ing 'em back to South Carol-liney by his-self."

The blacksmith looked at me. "Really?"

"His pard-nah got retired out of the busi-ness o'er in Canada."

"Uh-uh-uh. I'll do what I can. Brang 'em

'round back."

We pulled Syl's ma and pa to the back of the blacksmith's shop.

As soon as we was ten feet from the shop, the smells of the place started me feeling sick for home.

Once the blacksmith was finished with Syl's ma and pa, they was quite the sight.

He'd took the four-foot iron bar and put one end of the U that was on each end of it 'round the back of Syl's pa's neck. Next he put the front of Syl's ma's neck in the U at the other end of the bar. Then he run the chain through the holes in the ends of both of the Us.

Then he took some of the iron staples and hammered them so's Syl's parents couldn't slip out.

Next he pult off the cap'n's light shackles and put on the sheriff's heavy ones. But 'stead of bolting them down, he hammered more of the staples onto 'em.

It looked powerful bothersome.

Once the smithy was done, him and the sheriff walked out the shop.

Syl's pa said, "You know what that sheriff's man's got planned for you, don't you?"

"What you mean?"

"When you was out getting 'em shackles, he tolt the sheriff he wasn't 'bout to let three thousand dollars walk out his life without no fight. He done laid plans to bushwhack you on the way south."

Syl's ma joined in. "What you thinking, child? Can't you see you parading 'round with us is telling every scalawag 'twixt here and Carol-liney, 'All what stands 'twixt you and three thousand dollar is this dumb o'ergrowed sharecropper?'

"Can't you see the wolves is laying in wait? Don't you hear folk sharpening knives and waiting on you?"

My guts started aching something fierce when Syl's pa said, "Sheriff tolt Keegan he couldn't do nothing to y'all till you was out of Wayne County. Said he didn't want to have to write no reports 'bout no shallow graves being fount in the city."

"Why you telling me this?"

Syl's ma said, "We'd have a hard time with Keegan. And you" — she laughed — "I'm gonna have you talked outta this afore we gets outta Mitch-again. I seent your heart and I knows you ain't gonna do this."

My face was afire.

The sheriff come back in and said, "Look, boy. Iffen you's able to get 'em outta Deetroit, you might have a icicle's chance in the hot place, so I'm-a tell you what — you pay me for my time and my shackles and I'll see y'all to the city limits."

My seventh sense was burning.

The sheriff give Syl's ma and pa enough chain so's they could walk ten feet or so behind our horses.

If the sheriff hadn't been there, I don't think we'd've got off the first block.

We drawed some looks from colored folk and even some white ones that made the hair on my neck stand up.

One time the sheriff had to tell some folk, "Y'all move on; this here ain't none your business."

Another time he had to raise his shotgun and say, "Uh-uh, it ain't worth it. This is all legal. Papers is all good; ain't no one getting kidnapped."

By the time the streets had runned out and the buildings had gone from being giant walls to being brick to being wood to being only every once in the while, I was a nervous mess.

I near retched when the sheriff said, "All right, boy, what y'all gotta do is keep going due south on this trail 'bout four more mile; you gonna hit a town called River Rouge. Jus' 'bout there, you's gonna run back into the Dee-troit River; from there go di-rect south."

He shook his head and said, "Good luck.

241

Don't say I didn't warn you."

He turned north, and me and Syl's ma and pa kept south.

All the sudden every tree, every blade of grass, every pebble looked like it coulda been big 'nough for Keegan to be hiding behind.

I kept Pap's pistol gripped tight in my hand, relieved I hadn't had to use it on the sheriff.

Chapter 20

Never Looking Back

I wasn't sure which way we was gonna go, but it sure wasn't gonna be the way the sheriff said to. Soon's he disappeared on the road north, we made a sharp turn east through the woods, toward where I's thinking the river was. Meandering 'long the river would take lots longer, but it was the only way I could be sure we was gonna be heading south. And it also meant I wasn't gonna find Keegan behind the next bush.

Even though I knowed letting 'em go was the right thing to do, I kept having doubts. I always been tolt they ain't the same as us, they don't feel things like white people do, they don't love their kids the same, they don't love nothing but ducking work and sleeping. I always been tolt they ain't even got souls.

The big lie in that showed itself when I seent how Syl had falled so hard for that pretty girl. The only critter I'd ever seent that look on afore was a human being. And I ain't done much studying on the Bible, but I believe it do say somewhere in there that all human beings has souls.

Keegan and the Dee-troit sheriff and all them other folk wasn't 'bout to stop me.

We smelt the water long afore we come o'er a hill and seent it 'bout a half mile off.

There was a colored man sitting on the bank. He 'peared to have two lines in the water.

I tolt Syl's ma and pa, "I'm-a chain y'all to this tree and go down and talk to that colored man. You knows you ain't getting far with them shackles, so jus' be patient."

I wrapped the chain 'round a tree and left 'em.

I hoped they had sense 'nough not to run off with them heavy shackles on their necks.

I rode up on the man.

A rowboat was pult up on the riverbank next to him.

" 'Scuse me, sir, is this here the Dee-troit River?"

He didn't look up from his fishing pole.

"Sure is."

"How they biting?"

"Not bad; that cold winter we had means there's lots of perch."

"What you using?"

"Crawlers and minnerows."

I pointed 'crost the river.

"That there's Canada?"

"Uh-huh."

"You been there?"

"Many a time. Ain't gone far into it, though. Fishing's jus' as good here."

"How come you ain't using the rowboat?"

"I'm more comf-table being on land when I'm fishing. I live a couple miles downriver and this time of year the fishing's better up here."

"What's the best way to get o'er there?"

He looked at me.

"Whoo-wee! You took a good one, I see!"

"Yes, sir, got jumped by a whole mob."

"Looking to improve your luck in Canada, huh?"

"Maybe, sir."

"There's a ferry in Detroit, and one north of the city."

"How far's that?"

"Detroit?"

"Yes, sir."

"On horseback, it ain't but 'bout a hour

or so. And goodness me, what a horse that is!"

"Thank you, sir. Any blacksmiths 'tween here and the city?"

"Sure, Caleb Casement's 'bout half a hour down that road."

"Thank you, sir."

"You's quite welcome, son."

He stood and reached his right hand up to me.

We shook hands and he said, "My name's Johnny Norak. I gots some spare hardtack if you's hungry."

"I'm Charlie Bobo. No, thank you, sir. I needs to get back to Dee-troit."

He said, "Safe journeys, son."

"Thank you, sir."

I started Spangler back toward where Syl's folks was chained to the tree.

Something made me turn and ax him, "Sir, can that boat of yourn go to Canada?"

"Been there plenty; why you axing?"

"Jus' wondering."

"Be safe, son."

"You think your boat can carry three folk at the same time?"

He looked at me for a uncom-fitting long time afore he answered.

"Sure it can. No problem with that."

"You gonna be here for a while?"

He smiled. "Son, this river's fulla fish, but I'm-a do my best to empty it out. That ain't likely to be no quick job. Go 'bout your business; I'm-a be here a long time. And if you miss me today, I'm-a be back tomorrow."

Syl's ma and pa was where I'd left 'em, leaning so's the weight of the iron rod and chains was on the ground.

I thought 'bout the luck of the Bobos and seent that no matter how good I planned things out, it was probably a sure thing that this was gonna go bad for me real fast.

Syl's pa coulda picked up both me and Spangler and toss us into the next district. What if soon's I started taking 'em toward the blacksmith, he was to figger a way to take a rock, chuck it at me, and bash my head in?

Not only wouldn't they get free, but my life would be purt near ruint too.

Soon's they seent me, I tolt 'em, "Look, y'all. I know you's waiting to jump me and bash my head in. I'm begging you, please don't do nothing for another coupla hours or so.

"I swear on my pap's grave that I'm 'bout to turn y'all loose, but you gotta give me jus' a little more time."

They 'changed looks with each other and fought to get on their feet.

Syl's ma said, "You's 'bout to do what?"

"There's s'posed to be a blacksmith not far from here. Maybe I can pay him 'nough to get them chains took offen you. Jus' holt up on doing anything rough till we get to him. You give me your word?"

"What choice we got?"

"I can jus' let y'all go here, but if you swears you ain't gonna do nothing to me, I'll get them chains offen you."

Syl's pa said, "I give you my word."

I knowed Syl's ma could probably chuck a stone jus' as deadly as he could, so I said, "Ma'am?"

"I give you my word."

I tolt 'em, "And I give you my word too, and a Bobo's word is his bond."

They looked at each other and she said, "What's a Bobo?"

I didn't feel relaxed till we heard the blacksmith's hammer ringing out from somewhere 'head of us.

Syl's ma and pa heard it too. It was the first time I'd seent 'em smile.

When we got to the smithy, there was two kids playing out front of the shop.

Both kids ran screaming, "Father! Father,

come quick!"

The ringing of the hammer stopped and the smithy rushed out to see what had his chirren raising such a fuss.

They run right to him and shot me dirty looks from behind his legs.

Once he seent Syl's ma and pa, the smithy spit at the feet of Spangler and said, "I'll not be any part of chaining another human being, you filthy beast. Get off my property this minute or face the consequences."

Blacksmiths ain't to be meddled with; breathing in hot coals and hammering all day seem to make them not the most kindly folk you'll run into, and strong as they is, you don't want to take no chances on getting one of 'em vexed 'nough to take a poke at you. With or without a hammer.

I throwed my hands up and said, "Sir, I ain't looking to chain no one. I wants to know how much you gonna charge me to take their shackles offen 'em?"

Syl's ma was still giving me 'spicious looks.

The smithy said, "Are you jesting with me?"

"No, sir, I ain't taking no one back into that."

The smithy said, "There will be no charge. I'll be greatly pleased to free these people."

I turnt to Syl's ma and pa.

Her hand was covering her mouth.

She said to Syl's pa, "Chester, when we gets loose, you promise me you won't do nothing to him."

It took the blacksmith a hour of hard work to get the irons off Syl's ma and pa.

They rubbed their wrists and ankles. Their shoulders was already chafed raw and bloody.

I was right 'shamed at how only three or four hours in chains had done so much damage.

I tolt the blacksmith, "Sir, I ain't going through Dee-troit again; if the sheriff seent us, he'd grab these folk for hisself.

"There was a man fishing at the river; he tolt me his boat could go to Canada."

The smithy smiled and said, "That's Norak; he's a ferryman. He'll take them over with no problem. You think you might want to go too?"

"No, sir, I had me 'nough of Canada already. The parks is nice but the people's too peculiar and on edge for my tastes."

The smithy said, "Let's get everyone fed and we'll set off."

It was real uncom-fitting to sit and eat with the blacksmith's family and Syl's ma and pa.

After we was through, the blacksmith hitched a wagon for Syl's folks to ride in, and me and Spangler followed 'em down to the river.

The smithy rode with a double-barrel shotgun 'crost his lap.

Syl's ma said, "You's too soft for this game, boy. I ain't saying you can't be toughened up, but you ain't gonna never be no good at it. You ain't kilt the human part of yourself off yet. And after you done spent time with Cap'n Buck, that say there's something good 'bout you."

I was so relieved when we got to the river and Mr. Norak smiled and said, "I thought there was something 'bout you and all 'em questions, boy. Let's get these folk where they belong."

Syl's ma and pa thanked the blacksmith.

I counted out ten ten-dollar bills and handed 'em to Syl's ma.

She stared at 'em, then said, "Thank you, Little Charlie Bobo. You doing the right thing."

I had lots I wanted to say to her, but if you's responsible for putting heavy chains on someone's neck and trying to steal 'em back into being a slave, I don't think no 'pologies would ever get took to heart. I had to try anyway. I said, "Ma'am, sir, I'm sore shamed 'bout what I done."

She said, "If it wasn't for you, we wouldn't be free for the second time, boy. Don't be too hard on yourself."

I said, "There's a sheriff in Chat-ham name of Sudbury; he'll know where Syl's at."

They both said, "Thank you."

They clumb into the rowboat, and Norak the ferryman picked up the oars, set 'em in the locks, and said, "I ain't young as I once was; this might take some time. We's fighting 'gainst a mighty current."

Syl's ma and pa had their backs to us with their arms 'round each other's waists.

We watched 'em till they reached the other side.

I'll wonder for the rest of my life if things worked out OK.

The blacksmith said, "How old are you, son?"

"I'm gonna be thirteen in September, sir."

"So are you going to return to South Carolina?"

"I ain't sure, sir. I got some pondering to do. Ain't really no need to go back; our land's gone, ain't none of my family's still alive, and my dog's probably gone too. She's the best hunting dog in Richland District; someone's bound to have snatched her up.

"Plus, I don't know what Mr. Tanner's gonna feel about all this mess. I ain't keen to take no chance on getting whupped or hunged. Or cat-hauled."

"Well, you're welcome to stay with us for a bit."

"Thank you, sir. I truly 'preciate that. I can pay."

"No need for that. I do jus' fine. And you look like you ain't no stranger to hard work."

"No, sir, I ain't. I once plowed for twelve hours with a two-mule team, and I wasn't but ten year old, sir."

The boat reached the other shore. Syl's ma and pa got out and took to hugging and backslapping the ferryman.

He pointed 'em south.

Syl's ma and pa walked up the river's bank and disappeared into Canada.

They never once looked back.

If I was them, I wouldn't-a neither.

Epilogue

The Train Station, Buxton, Ontario
Canada West
September 25, 1858

The train hissed before jerking to a stop.

When the conductor lowered the steps onto the Buxton Station platform, only two figures, a man and a woman clinging to one another, were huddled in the door, hesitating before taking that final step.

Their glances were fleeting and frightened. They had the alertness of deer in the forest, ready to take flight at the least provocation. As they peeked out from the train, every movement on the station's platform drew their eyes in unison.

They stepped onto the platform as one.

The conductor cried, "All aboard!" and the train slowly creaked away.

Trying to get their bearings, the couple sidled to the eave at the station's southernmost point. They waited in silence.

Five minutes later, the door of the train station was hurriedly pushed open onto the platform as a group of six people, winded and obviously running late, surged out.

A young girl holding a sad brown sock doll preceded a tall young man, and a man and a woman, each carrying a child. Two girls. Twins.

The man and woman holding the twin girls set them down and directed their attention to the couple under the southern eave.

The twins fell apart; screaming "Mama!" they charged across the platform.

The teenage boy began to cry and followed them.

They were each snatched up and squeezed tight by the people waiting under the eaves.

Smiling, the girl holding the sock doll walked to the family.

Waiting until all eyes were on her, in a voice clear and strong she said, "Hello, my name is Emma Collins. I'm the first girl who was born free in Buxton.

"And now you're free too."

She extended her right hand.

"Come," she said, smiling. "We've been waiting for you."

AUTHOR'S NOTE

Let me say to the teachers who are reading this that I am aware of how important it is for writers, especially young writers, to outline before they start writing fiction. Otherwise there is a tendency for the writer to meander, to wander, to blindly flail around for the story.

My usual M.O. is to sit down and begin by imagining a character and a conversation. Then I start taking dictation. This is how I learn the character's personality, quirks, and capabilities. It is an effective way for me to get deep into his or her inner workings.

Even though there is no outline, most times when I start a novel I do have an idea where I want the story to go, but (and I've learned this through time and pain and struggle) if the story is a good one, it has a mind of its own and eventually it goes where *it* wants to. When this happens I'm pleased because I know I've tapped into something worthwhile. I've learned that instead of wrestling the writing back onto the road I want it to take, if I'm patient and listen carefully, the places where the story leads me always turn out to be the right places to go.

The hijacking of *The Journey of Little Charlie* happened quite early in this creative process.

The Journey of Little Charlie takes place in the southern United States and around the historically significant communities of Detroit, Michigan, and Chatham and Buxton, Ontario, Canada. I first became aware of Buxton and its outsized importance to both Canadian and American history while doing research for two other books, *Elijah of Buxton* and *The Madman of Piney Woods.*

Buxton had been set up in the swampy wilderness of southeast Canada as a haven for people who had escaped slavery in the southern US. It was no accident that the settlement was established in what was then a very remote part of Canada: Its placement was largely influenced by the Fugitive Slave Act of 1850, legislation passed by Canada's hugely powerful southern neighbour.

The act declared that when confronted by any white citizen, African Americans, even those in "free" states, had to present proof that they were not escaped slaves. If they were unable to produce the proper documentation, it was the duty of that white person to hold/arrest/kidnap them, which was the first step to being taken south and sold into servitude.

Slavery lasted 245 years in the United States of America because there were tremendous financial incentives to keep it in place. Slaves were the single most valuable asset in the American economy; the value of one individual ranged, in today's dollars, from $12,000 for a very young or very old field hand, to a staggering $176,000 for a skilled labourer.

One of the consequences of the Fugitive Slave Act was that Windsor, Ontario, which is separated from the United States only by the Detroit River, and which was once a safe haven for escaped former slaves, now became less safe. Many African Americans and African Canadians were kidnapped in Windsor and taken to the US to spend the rest of their lives enslaved. The slave narrative later made into the movie *Twelve Years a Slave* tells the story of one such free northern man who was kidnapped during a visit to Washington, DC. The settlement of Buxton was established east of Windsor, and deeper in the woods of Canada, so the escapees could live their lives unmolested and without the threat America posed.

Elijah of Buxton and *The Madman of Piney Woods* grew from my research into this small village that is such fertile ground for dramatic storytelling. I intended to set *Little Charlie* there as well, with even a few of the characters from the previous books playing small roles, but the story had other ideas.

In looking back over my notes for *Elijah of Buxton,* I came across an article published by Mary Ann Shadd Cary in a newspaper called the *Provincial Freeman* in September 1858. Shadd was the first woman of African descent to publish a newspaper anywhere in North America, and her daughter, Sarah Cary, makes an appearance in *The Madman of Piney Woods* as the owner of the Chatham print shop where Benji learns to write like a reporter. In the 1858 article, Shadd described a young African American boy whose family had lived in Canada for years who was (unbeknownst to him) being taken by train back into the US by a slave catcher. A white resident of London, Ontario, saw the two at a train station and became suspicious. He telegraphed ahead and, during its stop in Chatham, Ontario, the train was overtaken by a very large group of black and white people from Buxton and Chatham known as the Buxton Vigilance Committee. The boy, Sylvanus Demarest, was freed.

This article raised so many questions in my mind, chief among them this: How did this boy not know what was happening to him? Finding no other sources to research, I decided to answer my own questions by writing a novel about the incident, knowing nothing more about Sylvanus than his name.

So that's where I was going to go with *Little Charlie.* I was going to tell in alternating chapters the story of two boys: one black, Sylvanus Demarest, and one white, Little Charlie Bobo. I'd hoped to explore how much each was a product of his own environment and times, as well as to try and analyze what goes into making a human being do somethingcourageous.

My first step would be to catch the voices of the boys. I started writing the chapters Little Charlie would narrate first since it would be he who was going to have to make the longest journey.

But once I started pinning Little Charlie to the page, once I got to know his voice and personality, I knew this was *his* book. Sylvanus was going to have to wait.

I saw something in Little Charlie and knew, in spite of his circumstances and upbringing, that this was a character capable of doing something very brave, even heroic. But the story had other plans.

We're all heroes in our dreams. When looking back at some grand historical injustice I'm sure you've probably done as I have and said, "If I had been around at that time I would've . . ." Then you fill in the blank with whatever courageous, life-endangering action you would have taken to right this wrong.

Which is fine, except chances are good that that's pretty much a self-delusional lie.

The human condition is such that you and I would probably *not* be among the one-tenth-of-one-percent of people who really *would* initiate something brave. (Excuse my cynically low figure.)

No, we would be among the throng, the 99.9 percent who are quite content to either sit back and do nothing, or who at most would clench our teeth, furrow our brow, and say with great indignation, "Isn't that terrible?"

But it is that one-tenth-of-one-percent that is the stuff of great historic events and subsequently good fiction. When an author chooses to write in first person, the author develops a real closeness with the narrator; they become friendly. And after getting to know Little Charlie, I was convinced that even though he was raised awash in racism, ignorance, and all-encompassing poverty, he was a part of that brave minority.

Here was someone who was capable of seeing the lie of what he'd been taught. Here was someone who possessed great courage to which we all could aspire. Here was someone who, when presented with a great historic injustice, might have shaken his head and muttered, "Isn't that terrible?" — but instead of those words being the end of his reaction, they were the beginning, and he decided to cross a line, to step over into the ranks of the one-tenth-of-one-percent.

A step that is available to all of us.

ACKNOWLEDGMENTS

Many thanks to the people who read the manuscript for me and provided great suggestions: Dr. Rose Casement, Habon Curtis, Cydney Curtis, Rian Cocchetto, Jay Kramer, and Charlette White.

Huge thank-yous and "big ups" to two writers/readers who have supported and encouraged me since I first thought of myself as a writer: A. Corinne Brown and Janet Brown. In 1994, the Brown sisters were in the first and only writers' group I will ever belong to. In addition to being writing colleagues, I count them as great friends. Angela's background in literary criticism and Janet's perspective as a librarian with the Windsor Public Library have been most helpful in the writing of *The Journey of Little Charlie.* Their invaluable insights have made me a much better writer.

Thank you to Professor Richard J. Blackett at Vanderbilt University and to Chris

Tomlinson for lending their expertise.

And much gratitude to my many friends at Scholastic who have worked to make this book possible, with particular thanks to Joy Simpkins, Megan Peace, Deimosa Webber-Bey, Elizabeth Parisi, and especially to my editors Andrea Davis Pinkney and Anamika Bhatnagar.

ABOUT THE AUTHOR

Christopher Paul Curtis grew up in Flint, Michigan. His first novel, *The Watsons Go to Birmingham — 1963,* was awarded both a Newbery Honor and a Coretta Scott King Honor. His second novel, *Bud, Not Buddy,* won the Newbery Medal and the Coretta Scott King Award in 2000. *Elijah of Buxton,* the first of his Buxton Chronicles, was named a Newbery Honor Book, a Coretta Scott King Award winner, and a Canadian Library Association Book of the Year. His second Buxton novel, *The Madman of Piney Woods,* received four starred reviews. Christopher lives with his family in Windsor, Ontario. Visit him online at nobodybutcurtis.com.

The employees of Thorndike Press hope you have enjoyed this Large Print book. All our Thorndike, Wheeler, and Kennebec Large Print titles are designed for easy reading, and all our books are made to last. Other Thorndike Press Large Print books are available at your library, through selected bookstores, or directly from us.

For information about titles, please call:
(800) 223-1244

or visit our website at:
gale.com/thorndike

To share your comments, please write:
Publisher
Thorndike Press
10 Water St., Suite 310
Waterville, ME 04901